Tales from the Mermaid

A compilation of Nick Allen mysteries.

Allen Nicklin

'She is a mermaid but approach her with caution. Her mind swims at a depth most would drown in.'
J Iron Word

ISBN: 978-1-917293-67-9

Other books by Allen Nicklin

Winning the Benevolent Cup and Reaching First Base

Nick Allen and the Lost Boy

Nick Allen's Darkest Hour

In Memory of Paul Francis Dymond

28th January 1960 – 9 August 2022

I became friends with Francis (as he was known) about 20 years ago. With his broad Scottish accent and dry sense of humour, he became a regular and popular figure at the Mermaid Public House. His knowledge of all things Scottish and Scottish history was extensive, as was his interest in the Military. His good deeds included providing Christmas Dinners for the homeless on Christmas day. He was also very generous, donating beer related items for *Big Al's Bar* in my garden. **BUT** – it was only at the reception after his funeral that we discovered he was living a lie – he was English. He had us fooled for over 20 years. I met his best friend (a real Scot) a few weeks after the funeral, he looked at me, he hugged me, then said –

"He had a kind heart."

Contents

An Eye for an Eye

"And if a man causes a blemish in his neighbour;
as he hath done, so it shall be done to him."
Leviticus 24:19

An Eye for an Eye

14 November 1974

The pretty, petite woman entered the bar of the Plumber's Arms in Lower Belgrave Street at about 9.45 pm. People were able to remember the time because of the manner of her entry. She flung open the door and screamed. She was staggering and bleeding from head wounds and wearing a night-dress. She cried, 'Help me! Help me! I have just escaped from a murderer!' Then she began to weep. She went on to say, 'My children...my children...He's in the house...He's murdered the nanny...Help me!'

24 February 2004

Nick Allen sits in the bar of the Mermaid public house, nursing a sore head trying to decide whether to have another pint of Oscar Wilde. It is 3.00pm on a damp, miserable afternoon in February. At only 3.7% this dark mild from the Mighty Oak brewery in Essex has a coffee and chocolate taste which definitely satisfies his palate. Why, you may ask, is he drinking at this time in the afternoon and not toiling away in some office or factory and doing his bit for society. Simple really; he has been suspended from his position as Lecturer in Mathematics at the St Albans Regional College, which as it happens, is only 25 yards away from this pub. Also, you may ask why he is nursing a sore head. To answer this question, one must explain the events of the last seven days and why he was in this pub at the same time last Tuesday.

Nick Allen is 54 years old and has been teaching at the college for 28 years. He lost his wife Jane, in a car accident six months ago and has struggled on his own ever since. It is difficult to comprehend how the accident happened, as she was a very good driver. The report suggested that she lost control and hit a tree on Coopers Green Lane, St. Albans. He has been diagnosed with mild depression and the pills he has been prescribed do not seem to work. This may be because he has not actually taken them. Therefore, you can understand that work has not been easy for

3

him. Students, staff, in fact most people were getting on his nerves. He was as taut as a bow string and ready to snap at any moment. Normally, he is a placid man, patient with the students and willing to help his teaching colleagues. In fact, he was known all round as a good egg. But there is always one, that little turd who gets right up your nose. In this case the turd was called Mark Robertson. He works in the I.T. department, and some sort of course coordinator. Nick teaches one of his classes Key Skills Numeracy. Normally this course would run for 30 weeks, each lesson lasting one hour. Due to some cock-up in the timetable this class had a free lesson after his. So, the head of I.T. decided that the lesson should be extended to two hours. He argued against this with his line-manager but to no avail. Unfortunately, he was lumbered teaching a nice group of lads a subject that they were not really interested in for twice as long. It was agreed with the students that he would teach formally for seventy-five minutes, then they would go to the Learning Centre to research and work on their assignment. A perfect situation for both parties. Mr. Nice Guy strikes again or so he thought. Unfortunately, his problems began when he received an e-mail from his line manager, who sits no more than six feet away, enquiring why he was dismissing the class in question early? He noticed that this e-mail originated from the turd. He had first sent the query to his boss; she had sent it to Nick's boss who in turn had sent it to Nick. What an arse about face way of doing things; if he had a problem why not approach him first? Nick was incensed, so straight away he emailed the turd stating that if he has a problem come and talk to me. The email then went on to say it's all about communication and perhaps he should brush up on his man-management skills. In hindsight he thought that the email was a mistake; but at the time it made him feel better.

It is important that the reader should know that Nick has never actually met Mark Robertson. He knows what he looks like, and he knows him by reputation. A man with 'Short Person Syndrome' - '*an angry male of below average height who feels it necessary to act out in an attempt to gain respect and recognition from others and compensate for his abnormally short stature*'. To compensate for his lack of stature he wears Cuban heeled boots. Unfortunately, they make his body lean forward i.e. an angle of 70° to the ground. His nose appears in the room five seconds before his feet. It's a standing joke at the college.

Anyway, Nick's boss, June Thomas, Head of Mathematics, a cross between Penelope Keith and Joyce Grenfell, called him into her office and they agreed that Nick should teach the class for the full two hours. Minor bollocking, no problem, end of story; little did he know. As it happens, the class was seen by Mark Robertson at 10.30 am. He asked them what they were doing and one of the students asked him why they couldn't start at 10.00 am instead of having to wait till 11.15 am for the next lesson. Nick's lesson started at 9.00 am, tea break from 11.00 till 11.15.

Weekends are the worst when you are alone, especially Sundays. Nick can cope with Saturdays; he has a lie in, reads the papers, and drinks lots of coffee. He usually has a wander around the market, pops to the pub at about 1.00 pm for a few beers, watches some football being shown on Sky Sports. If a few of his mates were around he would stay in the pub and watch the 5.30 pm game. Pick up a take-away on the way home, hit the Laphroaig whisky, watch Match of the Day, and hit the sack. So, on Sundays he might have a slight hangover which is not a good start when it is the only day he gets to do household chores. Clean a few rooms, do a bit of washing, ironing and tidy the garden. In the afternoon he might put on a DVD to try and cheer himself up. In truth he just sits there and feels sorry for himself and thinks that the Laphroaig will go off if he doesn't drink it soon.

As mentioned, the class in question was his first lesson Monday morning and he was not in a particularly good mood. The lesson started as it normally does. 'Can I borrow some paper', 'I've forgotten my pen', 'my sister's nicked my calculator' and the rest. He always brought a pad, a few pens, and a box of calculators. It saves all the hassle of moaning at them, so they get some work done. Even when stressed Nick is a patient person, but everyone has that button. Press the button and you explode. Unfortunately for one student he did not knowingly hit the button.

'What time are we packing up sir? He asked.

Nick turned away from the board, put his pen down. 'What fucking time do you want to finish?' he shouted.

Their mouths dropped.

'What are you trying to do? Get me the fucking sack. You report me for letting you go early, and then you want to know what time I'm letting you go. We agreed that you could finish early, I was doing you a favour, and this is how you treated me. Do I report you for coming in late, not having the right equipment? No, because I'm the good guy here and you lot are just a bunch of tossers. In my day I would have taken you behind the bike shed and given you a good thrashing.'

Nick walked out of the class and went back to his office. He has a bottle of Jack Daniels in his filing cabinet, for emergencies and medicinal purposes. Nick returned to the class five minutes later, they were still there. He continued the lesson as if nothing had happened.

Nothing much happened for the rest of the week, nothing was said, and everything was calm. It wasn't until Friday evening that the shit hit the fan. He'd finished teaching at 3.00 pm and for once didn't fancy a drink before he went home. Feeling hungry, he found a Tesco Tikka Masala meal for one and put it in the microwave. He might pop out for a beer later. It was just after five o'clock when the doorbell rang. Nick answered it and standing there was Paul Vickers, Personnel Manager of St Albans Regional College. A man most would describe as a slug; in his mid -fifties, overweight, greasy grey hair, wearing a dull grey suit.

'Hello Nick,' he said.

Nick didn't reply.

'I must inform you that you have been suspended. You have been accused of swearing at and threatening students. I have all the details here.'

He passed Nick a A4 brown envelope.

'There will be an investigation and we will let you know when the hearing will be. In the meantime, you are not allowed on college premises, and you are not to communicate with any member of staff.'

With that he turned and walked away. Nick stood there stunned, then turned, walked back into the house, and slumped onto the sofa.

What the hell's going on, he thought.'

Pulling himself together, he opened the envelope, took out the contents and read.

Dear Mr. Allen.

It has been reported to management that you have behaved in a totally unacceptable way towards a class of students. This behaviour could constitute gross misconduct if the report is substantiated, which would result in your dismissal without notice.

Your curriculum Manager Alice Williams has been appointed by the college to investigate the report. Whilst this report is being investigated you will be suspended from duty on full pay pending the conclusion of this matter.

You should not attend college or contact any member of staff or students during this period of suspension, other than your trade union representatives, if you are a member.

The investigating officer, giving reasonable notice, will invite you to an interview to give you the opportunity to respond to the allegations being made against you. You may be accompanied by a friend at this interview, which is part of the investigation and may be used as evidence at a disciplinary hearing.

You have the right to appeal against the principal's decision to suspend you if the suspension lasts for longer than three weeks. Unfortunately, investigations can take longer but I undertake to update you on the progress at three weekly intervals.

You will be informed of the outcome of the investigation, which will either be to proceed no further or hold a disciplinary hearing.

I would stress that at this stage no assumption of guilt has been made but that a report has been made, which needs to be investigated. The principal has confirmed that in these circumstances suspension is appropriate.

Every effort will be made by the college to keep this matter confidential. I enclose a copy of the Disciplinary Procedure for your information.

If you have any queries about this process, please do not hesitate to contact me.

Yours sincerely
Paul Vickers.

Nick panicked, his breathing increased, and he started pacing up and down the hall. He could feel his heart pounding in his chest. 'Get a grip, get a grip,' he kept saying to himself. He went to the drinks cabinet and poured himself a very large Laphroaig. After a few minutes, things calmed down. The first thing to do is phone my union representative. Who is my union representative? Ah yes, I remember, Howard South, how do I contact him? Phone him at work. No good, he would have gone home by now. Phone him at home, don't know his number. Check the phone directory, don't know where he lives. Phone the college and get his number.

Nick phoned the college and asked to be put through to the personnel office. It was 5.25pm, he might just catch them. Someone picked up.

'Hello, personnel here, can I help you?'

'Hi,' he replied. 'This is Nick Allen from the Math's Department; can you give me Howard South's home phone number?'

'Sorry we are not allowed to give out that sort of information'.

'Listen, he's my union representative, this is an emergency, and I need to contact him.'

'As I said, we are not allowed to give out that sort of information'.

'So, what am I supposed to do?'

'Try looking him up in the phone book.'

'What a great idea,' he said sarcastically.' 'What is his address?'

'I'm sorry we are not allowed to give out that sort of information'.

8

'Thanks for nothing,' Nick replied and slammed the phone down.

I need a drink; this could be a heavy session. Storming out, Nick grabbed his bike out of the shed and pedaled the two miles to the Mermaid public House.

The Mermaid public house was built in the nineteenth century and has been described as a 'community pub'. Formally it consisted of two bars, a Public and a Lounge bar but now is just one 'L' shaped bar. Nick had been drinking in this pub on and off since he was big enough to convince the landlord that he was 18 years old. As mentioned earlier it is situated across the road from the college and very near to the town centre, so the clientele is varied, but you get to know the regulars. Nick described it as the St Albans version of 'Cheers', where everyone knows your name. Nick is affectionately referred to as 'Ol' Nick'. The landlord is called Ken, a jovial chap, in his thirties, long hair in a ponytail. Always wore jeans and a brewery tee shirt.

Notable characters in the pub that evening were Angus Gold, late forties, five foot ten, lean, going grey and sporting a goatee beard. Works in mental health, very intelligent, warped sense of humour, loves military warfare and all things Scottish. Very friendly, Nick liked him a lot, and they got on well. Talking to him was Rodney Black, early forties, five foot seven, normal build, fair hair, in-between jobs; another nice lad. Nick joined them, checked out the guest beers and choose a pint of *Moorhouse's Pendle Witches Brew*. It was the strongest available at 5.1%. He didn't offer to buy them one as both their glasses were almost full.

Angus was the first to speak 'What's up laddie, you look as miserable as sin.'

'Just been suspended, don't want to talk about it,' Nick replied.

'Yes, you do,' Rodney said. 'Otherwise, you wouldn't have come in here'.

Nick gave a big sigh and spent the next fifteen minutes pouring his heart out to them.

'So, what are you going to do about it?' asked Rodney.

'Well, there's not much I can do 'till Monday. This is so stupid; I really don't need this now. What I do need is another drink, what are you having? Landlord, when you are ready.'

'I think I was next old chap.'

Nick looked behind him. It was 'Posh Ron', an elderly gentleman in his seventies, tall, shaggy beard with a very upper-class accent. He had been drinking here for a few months now. Keeps himself to himself, always drinks large malts. Sits alone reading the Times; usually leaves about six thirty.

'Sorry Ron didn't see you there', Nick replied.

'Need another one urgently; it feeds the old grey matter. Today's crossword is particularly difficult.'

Ron was quickly served, and he went back to his seat and attempted to complete the crossword.

'Bloody English aristocrat, who does he think his,' Angus was back on his high horse. 'Ah, who does he think he is? Can't stand the bastard; I know his sort; think they own the place. Did I ever tell you what they did after the Battle of Culloden in 1746? Outrageous; I'll never forgive them.'

'Angus,' Nick said. 'That was over two hundred years ago, and you weren't even there.'

'That's not the point; history is full of examples of English oppression, especially against us Scots'.

'Okay, we are all bastards, but can we get back to my problem?'

'Alright; but he looks old enough to have been there.'

'Whatever'.

A group of Art lecturers were sitting at a table enjoying their end of the week drink. They looked over and waved. Nick wondered what they would say when the news broke on Monday. The rest of the evening was spent with light-hearted banter, Nick left about 9:00. He managed to cycle home without falling off. After a quick wash he went straight to bed and spent a troubled night dreaming about hordes of invading Scots raping and pillaging the Personnel department at St Albans Regional College.

Tuesday 17 February 2004

The weekend passed without incident, and Monday Nick spent the morning on the phone to his Union representative. They arranged a meeting for the following Friday. Nick was told to write down everything he could remember about the incident and the events leading up to it. Howard said he would sniff around and let Nick know if he found out anything. Nick spent the rest of the day and most of Tuesday preparing his statement before venturing to the Mermaid at about 4.00 pm.

Angus and Rodney were in their usual position at the bar, both with pints of lager. They were joined by another relatively new punter called Terry. He was tall, about six foot two, athletic build, late thirties early forties, difficult to tell. Brown hair, slightly receding, talked with a London accent. Rumour has it he was a project manager in IT and was staying at a local hotel weekdays and going back to London at the weekends. Posh Ron was in his usual seat with his large malt, reading the Times. Nick joined them but wasn't feeling very talkative, so he picked up a copy of the Sun and turned to *Dear Deidre*. Maybe someone else's life is worse than his. The *Photo Casebook* was showing some chap bonking both his girlfriend and her mother. Which one did he really love? What if his girlfriend finds out? Who writes this shit? Mental note: buy a copy tomorrow and find out.

At about 6.00 pm Angus says he must pop back to his office as he has forgotten something. A minute later Rodney states that he has run out of cat food so he would nip to Tesco's before it shut. Then Terry decided he needed a cigarette and went outside.

'Cracked it,' shouted Posh Ron. He downed the last few drops of his malt whisky, put on his hat and coat; said goodbye and left.

Some joker had selected *Alone again (Naturally)* by Gilbert O'Sullivan on the jukebox. *Typical* Nick thought and sat there thinking about his wife Jane. God how I miss her; what would she have thought of this mess. She would have been very supportive, but not before I received a lecture on all the idiots who worked at the college. How I could have done better for myself and how I should sue their arses. They had been married for over thirty years, childhood sweethearts. They had two daughters, both grown up and moved away. He didn't want to trouble them with his problems. He'll tell them when it is all over.

Still feeling depressed, he ordered another pint of *Augustinian* from the *Nethergate Brewery*. A particular favourite of his and at 4.5% it is just right for a session. When you are feeling down the only thing to cheer you up is a few songs by Leonard Cohen. He walked over to the juke box and searched out all the Leonard Cohen songs he could find for two pounds. *Suzanne* was there, so was *Bird on a Wire* and *So Long Marianne*. He eventually found his favourite *Chelsea Hotel No 2*. He loves the story he tells about this song. He says he was in the Chelsea Hotel in New York when he met Janice Joplin in the lift. She said that she was looking for Kris Kristofferson and he replied, 'it's your lucky day I'm Kris Kristofferson.' Nick's favourite line is '*She told me again that she preferred handsome men, but for me she would make an exception'*. *Who by Fire, Sisters of Mercy* and *The Partisan* made up his seven choices. Deep in thought, he remembered a T Shirt he saw a man wearing once, it said, 'Sad songs make me happy'. Mental note: must buy one sometime.

At about 6.30 pm Nick heard a police siren wiz passed the pub, a common occurrence in St Albans. He thought nothing of it until someone rushed into the pub saying that a body had been found battered in the churchyard. The few remaining drinkers all got to their feet and rushed out of the door. It was dark outside, not too cold for the time of the year and drizzling slightly. It was easy to spot the blue flashing light about 100 yards to the left. They ventured up, on the opposite side of the road and stood there looking. There wasn't much to see, the police had taped of the alley that led to the church yard between the Museum and the old church hall. They waited around for a while, but they couldn't see anything, so they all wandered back to the pub. It was about 8.30 pm; Nick was just thinking of going home as none of his original drinking partners had returned, when Detective Sergeant Keith Blakely walked in. Nick had seen him in here a few times, mainly during the lunch hour, and they were on nodding terms. Rumour has it that he was a good detective but as normal had a drink problem which had put a halt to any promotion. He looked at Nick. Nick smiled back.

'Any chance of a chat?' he asked.

'No problem,' Nick replied. 'Is it official?'

'Why do you ask that?' he snapped.

'Well, if it isn't I'll buy you a drink.'

'Oh, yer right. Umm, well yes and no.'

'Whatever. Jameson's, is it?' Nick rose and went to the bar. Ken the landlord was serving.

'Jameson's, large one.'

Ken smiled. 'Gonna get him talking are yer?' he asked, suppressing a smirk.

'Well, why not? Just might get some useful titbits about the murder.'

'If it was a murder,' said Ken, 'don't jump the gun.'

Nick smiled and paid for the drink then returned to his seat. 'So, who was murdered?'

'It looks like Posh Ron, but we'll need a formal identification,' he replied.

'Bloody Hell,' Nick felt sick. 'What happened?'

'Seems he was on his way home, he was attacked. Head was bashed in.'

'Were there any witnesses? Did you find the weapon? Was he robbed?'

'Hang on a minute,' DS Blakely snapped. 'I'm the one supposed to be asking the questions.'

'Sorry,' Nick replied, 'just making conversation'.

'Of course you are. Don't think I don't know about your reputation.'

'I'm sure I have no idea what you are talking about,' replied Nick with a smirk.

'Don't give me that, anyway its thirsty work this interviewing,' he said looking down at his empty glass.

'Same again then?' Nick asked.

He just smiled and pushed his empty glass towards Nick. Ken had already poured the drink as he arrived at the bar.

'How's it going?' he asked.

'At this rate you'd better get another bottle ready.' Nick replied before returning to his seat.

'Now, let me ask you a few questions,' Blakely said as he took a large sip of his whisky. 'Did you see Posh Ron in this pub this evening?'

'Yes, I did.'

'And?'

'And what?'

'What time did he leave, was he followed, did you see nothing suspicious?'

'Just after 6.00, no, no.'

'Is that it?' He seemed agitated.

'What else do you want me to say?'

He raised his eyebrows.

'What was his real name?' Nick asked enthusiastically.

He gave a big sigh. 'His real name was Ron DuCall.'

Now we were getting somewhere. 'Any family?'

'No more questions,' he snapped. 'Now let me get this straight. He was in there as usual, drinking on his own and he left some time just after six. Is that right?'

'Correct.'

'Is there anything else you can remember?'

'Yes. He finished his crossword,' Nick smiled.

'God help us,' and with that he rose and went to question some other drinkers.

Ron DuCull, thought Nick, unusual name, must google it tomorrow. He was just about to leave when Colin Grande walked in.

'Have I missed something?' he enquired.

'Sit down mate and I'll tell you all the gossip. What do you want?'

'Cider please.'

Nick called over to Ken, 'Cider please and same again for me.'

Colin is a couple of years younger than Nick, but they go back a long way. They were involved in running a local football team and they regularly turned out for their veterans' team. Nick used to kick the ball and Colin kicked ankles. He recently retired from his job as Project Manager and had turned his hand to pig farming. He now owns a healthy herd of Gloucester Old Spot. During mid-conversation they were interrupted by Kate, the local alcoholic. Kate, who is about thirty, is a tragic case. Her husband walked out on her two years ago when she found him in bed with her best friend. Rumour has is that after screaming at the pair, she asked 'what's she got that I haven't?' He replied, 'what apart from bigger tits and a nicer arse?' The pair moved out of the area and Kate hit the bottle.

'What's a couple of good-looking guys like you doing sitting alone in this crappy pub?'

'Piss off,' said Colin.

'Ooo, playing hard to get ah?'

'So,' Nick intervened, 'how's it going Kate?'

'I've got an interview tomorrow for a job. PA.'

'That's good,' he said, trying to show interest. 'What company?'

'Tesco. They are interested in my creative and artistic talents.'

'In other words – a shelf stacker,' said Colin sarcastically. 'Heard from your husband lately?'

Kate started to cry.

'Don't start sniveling, he was only joking. Come on let me buy you a drink.' *I'm too soft*, thought Nick.

'Thank you.' she sniffed. 'Vodka and coke, large one.'

'Ken,' he called. 'Vodka and large coke.'

'I used to be a model; you know.'

'Oh yeh,' said Colin. 'The new Twiggy were yer?'

I wasn't always this thin; I've just lost my appetite. Anyway, I know who murdered Posh Ron.'

'And who would that be?' Nick asked.

'It was Angus. I saw him hanging around that alley; you know where they found the body.'

'That's cos his private office is down there, you silly cow' screamed Colin.

'That may be so, but that nice policeman thought it was interesting, he bought me a drink.'

With that she gulped down her vodka and coke then turned to walk away.

'I could have shown you two a good time,' she smiled and went in search of her next free drink.

'Look on the bright side Colin,' Nick said. 'It's not often you get propositioned by a women twenty years younger than yourself. Think of your street cred.'

'I think I'd rather shag one of my pigs,' he replied, 'same again?'

15

Wednesday 18 February 2004

Although Nick had had a skin full, sleep didn't come easy. He was thinking about poor Ron. He seemed harmless enough, but did he have enemies? Angus certainly didn't like him, and he wasn't in the pub when the evil deed was committed. Then again neither was Terry nor Rodney. Come to think of it, hundreds of people weren't in the pub at 6.00pm last night. Nick thought *'wouldn't it be great if I could solve the murder'*. Well, it would at least take his mind off his other problem. He eventually drifted off to sleep and had another restless night. This time he dreamt he was chasing Angus, who was dressed in his complete highland regalia down the High Street. Nick was wearing a deer stalker and a cape, and Angus was shouting that he did it for Scotland and death to all Sassenachs.

Nick decided to visit the Mermaid at lunchtime to see if DS Blakely was there so he could ask him for more information. As it happens, he was there, propping up the bar looking as if he had all the world's troubles on his shoulders.

'D.S. Blakely, me ol' mate, how's it hanging,' Nick greeted him with the old arm round the shoulder routine.

'Oh, it's you; what do you want?'

'Don't be like that,' Nick replied. 'Let me fill that up for you. Ken!' I shouted 'Another Jameson's' for my friend. So, how's the investigation going?'

'Slowly,' he sighed. 'We found the murder weapon, a brick, it had come loose from the wall, and they used that. No prints.'

'So,' Nick enquired, 'any more facts about the victim?'

'Not a lot, which is strange really. We searched his room but didn't find much personal stuff. Checked our records, no trace of any family; recently returned to England after living in South Africa for the forty odd years. Also, no fingerprints to check; he seemed to have had some sort of industrial accident on his hands, very odd. But I shouldn't be telling you stuff like, so no more questions.'

'No problem, I'll leave you to enjoy your drink.'

Nick moved away and ordered a pint of *Sarah Hughes Dark Ruby Mild*, at 6% this should get my 'little grey cells' working. He'd read recently somewhere that the personification of mild is someone who has depth, tends to be misunderstood, provokes a knee-jerk action, and should be revisited as many times as it takes to understand their greatness; just like Leonard Cohen or me.

Nick took out his notebook and looked at the name Ron DuCall. Strange name: he recalled that people who change their name use the same initials or perhaps rearrange it. Seems they like a small link to their original identity. He was just finishing off his third pint, when it hit him. Oh....my.... god. That's impossible. He looked again; it is. Wow, if this is right, I have stumbled on a mystery that has gripped the nation for nearly forty years. This calls for some serious googling.

Nick grabbed his coat, rushed outside, and managed to cycle home without too much difficulty. His head was spinning, a mixture of intoxication and excitement, but he managed to focus on his web search and after a couple of hours he had formulated a plan of action.

Thursday 19 February 2004
Nick's mobile started ringing as he was enjoying his breakfast of honey on toast. It was Rodney.

'They've arrested Angus,' he exclaimed.

'When?' It was all Nick could think of saying.

'Yesterday afternoon, they kept him in overnight, and they gave me a right grilling yesterday as well.'

'Why?' Nick replied, 'what have you done?'

'Well, I wasn't exactly telling the truth when I said I was buying cat food, they checked.'

'Right, so what were you doing?'

'You don't want to know. I'll tell you later. It's a long story. Are you up the pub lunchtime?'

'No, I have business in London. It might help to save Angus.'

'Interesting, okay I'll see you when you get back.'

'Maybe, see you,' Nick ended the call.

He finished his breakfast and prepared for his London trip. Nick then cycled to the station and bought a one-day travel card and waited for the old BedPan train. (Bedford to St Pancras). After reaching St Pancras he transferred to the Victoria line and boarded a tube train for Victoria. He exited the tube station opposite the Apollo Theatre. A big sign indicated that they were

17

staging 'Wicked' there. *I must see that show soon.* Nick maneuvered his way through all the tourists and travelers and found Buckingham Palace Road. His destination was Lower Belgrave Street, just on the right. It didn't take too long to find what he was looking for, *The Plumbers Arms* public house. This 19th century pub was built by the builder Thomas Cubitt and was named in honour of the tradesmen who helped build the magnificent houses that surround it. The pub consisted of just one bar, typical Victorian style with wood panels and little alcoves. Nick checked out the Real Ales and ordered a pint of *Celt Golden* Crafted Ale. He also ordered a Chicken and Bacon sandwich in white bloomer. He took a sip of his beer, it wasn't too bad, then turned and looked at the clientele. The pub wasn't crowded but most tables were taken. *I must be careful who I choose.* Nick's luck was in; sitting in the corner by himself was an elderly gentleman, smartly dressed, maybe late sixties or early seventies hard to tell. He walked over to his table.

'It's a bit crowded may I join you?' Nick asked.

'If you like,' he replied.

'Nice pub,' Nick said, pretending to take an interest in the surroundings.

'It's okay.'

'Been drinking here long?' Nick enquired.

'Since twelve o'clock, when it opened'.

'Very good,' Nick laughed. 'I meant.......'

'I know what you mean. Are you a journalist?'

'Do I look like a journalist?'

'What does a journalist look like?'

'No idea. I was just making conversation.'

He smiled, 'or are you just one of the Ghouls interested in the murder?'

He's not stupid, Nick thought. 'Actually, I'm interested in historical pubs and, if they are connected to a murder, all the better. I've visited the '*Magdala*' in Hampstead, you know the Ruth Ellis connection. The '*Blind Beggar*', the Krays; and the '*Ten Bells*', Jack the Ripper. So naturally this one was next.'

'I knew her,' he whispered, 'you know Sandra, the girl who was murdered.'

'Did you, now that is interesting,' Nick replied. 'I've done a little research; I believe she had two sons, Stephen and Gary?'

'That's what they all think,' he smiled, 'actually, she had a third son. He was adopted by her sister Theresa; they called him Terry.'

'Wow,' Nick exclaimed, 'what happened to him?'

'Now that is an interesting question, because I've seen him in here a few times over the past few months. He was always a bit strange. When he found out whom his real mother was, he vowed to find the killer and kill him. Well, everybody knows that the real killer must be dead by now.'

'So, what was he doing in here then?' Nick asked.

'Well, he's always in here with a couple of mates; in fact, you have only just missed him.'

'And who were they?' Nick was getting excited now.

'Those two at the bar who have been giving you evil looks since you sat down.'

Nick discreetly looked around and saw two hefty men dressed smartly in suits in deep conversation. When he'd finished his pint and sandwich and said goodbye to the old gentleman Nick made his way out of the pub. He turned right and made his way through Belgravia. He thought he would see how the other half lived then pick up a tube at Knightsbridge. He hadn't been walking for long when he sensed that he was being followed. Nick glanced round and sure enough there were the two heavies from the pub. They soon caught up with him, so he turned quickly round to face them.

'What?' said Nick.

'We would like a quick word.' said the one to his right.

'Fast, that's a quick word, will that do?'

'Don't try and be funny,'

Nick shrugged his shoulders, 'sorry, you asked.'

'Don't go messing into things that don't concern you,' said the one to his left.

'Are you threatening me?' asked Nick.

They moved a little closer, they were a little taller than Nick, maybe an inch or two, well built; looked like they worked out regularly. *What would Reacher do here*? Thought Nick. As it happened, Nick was a Black Belt in Shotokan Karate. Make it quick and decisive. He slowly raised his arm and combed his hair with his fingers, then swiftly elbowed the guy to his right in the face. The second guy turned to see what happened and was caught full in the face with his fist. They both fell to their knees. Both men down in less than two seconds, Jack would have been proud. Nick was shaking, but still in control as he ran towards Belgrave Square Gardens. When they were out of sight he stopped running, well he thought that was an adrenalin rush. Nick followed the road until it met Knightsbridge, then turned left, and made his way to the tube station.

Nick didn't go out that night; he put on a Chris De Burgh CD, *The Love Songs,* and poured himself two fingers of Laphroaig. So, he thought. If Terry is Sandra's third son, he could be the killer. Do I report it to DS Blakely or try to find Terry myself. He came up with two logical reasons for not telling him. One, I don't think he would believe me; two, with all their resources I'm sure they already know. So tomorrow I'll track down Terry. I've had enough excitement for one day.

Friday 20 February 2004
The best place to start looking for Terry would be at the Mermaid. So, he made his way there at about 1.00pm to catch the lunchtime crowd. He ordered a cheese and ham sandwich with crisps and a pint of *Colley's Dog* from the *Tring Brewery* at 5.2%. Rodney was in and Nick joined him.
'How's the job search going?' Nick enquired.
'Not bad,' he replied. 'Got a few irons in the fire.'
'Seen Terry lately?'
'Funny that,' he said. 'I haven't seen him since Tuesday. Normally he's in here most lunch times, and most evenings.'
'Do you know where he's staying?' asked Nick.
'No, I didn't think to ask, can't be far away.'
'Who do you think would know?'
He thought for a while.
'He's always talking to June; she's bound to know.'
June was the part-time barmaid, early forties, and some would call her voluptuous, others overweight, platinum blonde. Good worker, always friendly. Rodney ordered another round which

gave Nick a chance to question her. 'Do you know where Terry is staying?'

'He never told me.' she replied. 'But I did once see him go into the *Ardmore* Hotel just round the corner'.

'I know it, my sister-in-law used to stay there when she visited us from America. Run by Italians.'

Nick finished his drink and told Rodney he had some business to attend to and he'd see him back here in about an hour.

It was about a half a mile walk to the hotel, just enough time for Nick to formulate another plan. He didn't know Terry's surname, which could be a problem when asking if he was staying there and which room he was occupying. Nick remembered that they did have a bar there, so that was his first call. The bar was empty; he pulled up a stool and waited. A young Italian girl eventually appeared and asked nick what he would like.

'Peroni please.'

'No problem,' she replied in a strong Italian accent.

'I'm meeting Terry here for a drink, I'm a little early.'

'Mister Terry has just booked out; he is leaving us today'.

'Has he left the hotel?' Nick asked.

'Not yet, he is just finishing packing.'

'In that case I'll pop along to his room. What number is he?

'He's in room 16, through the dining room in the annex.'

Nick followed her instructions and easily found the room; he knocked on the door.

Terry opened the door, and he didn't look surprised to see him.

'I was expecting you last night,' he said ushering Nick in.

'Sorry to disappoint you,' Nick replied. As he turned to face him, he noticed there was pointing a gun at him. Reacher would now describe the gun, but they all look the same to Nick. Not that he's seen many guns; well, none actually, only on the television.

'Sit down.'

Nick obliged.

'I'm interested to know what put you on to me.' Terry asked.

'A few things really, the first was when you left on Tuesday night you said you were popping out for a cigarette. It didn't strike me for a couple of days but then I remembered you don't smoke.'

'Silly mistake,' he replied.

'Then once I'd figured out who Posh Ron really was. All I needed to do was find a motive. That's when I went to the *Plumbers Arms*. After that it was, as you would say *'Elementary my dear Terry.'*

'Yes, I heard that you met my mates.'

'And how are they?' Nick asked with a large smirk on my face.

'Julian has a depressed fracture of the cheekbone and Charles has a broken nose.'

'I'm pleased about that.'

'So, how did you find out Posh Ron's real identity?'

'Easy, it was just an anagram, but how did you find out?'

He sat down in front of Nick, still pointing the gun, took a deep breath and told me. 'After murdering my mother, he fled to Sussex, some friends hid him away until they could arrange a private plane to smuggle him to France. He stayed there for a few months whilst his influential friends could arrange a new identity for him. When all the paperwork had been completed, he went to South Africa where he has lived ever since. But in the last few years he had become homesick so his friends arranged for him to come back to England and live out his remaining days somewhere quiet, someplace where no one would recognize him. So, they chose St Albans.'

'Fascinating,' Nick said, 'but where do you fit in?'

'Julian's dad is a member of the 'committee' that arranged his comeback. Julian overheard them planning his return and told me. It didn't take long to track him down. I have been watching him for weeks. Once I had established a pattern of his movements the rest was easy. I knew he always walked through the churchyard after his evening tipple. So, I just waited for him and…. well, you know the rest,'

He stood up, still pointing the gun. Nick felt helpless.

'Well, as nice as it was talking with you, I have to go.'

'You'll never get away with it,' Nick replied.

'Same old cliché,' he sneered.

He walked behind and hit Nick on the head with the gun. Nick passed out.

The weekend and Monday

Nick vaguely remembers coming round in the ambulance, but it wasn't till Saturday morning that he was fully conscious. He had a blinding headache and eight stitches. The doctor said he was lucky his skull wasn't cracked. Apparently, Nick has very dense bones. His first visitor was his daughter Sarah who was there first thing. She insisted that Nick go and stay with her as soon as he was released. Nick didn't want to tell her about his other problem, but thought it was best to. She gave him a right good lecture; her mother would have been proud. The next visitor was DS Blakely. Nick gave him his statement; he gave Nick a rollicking saying that he should pass all information to the police. Nick argued that they wouldn't have taken him seriously and then he went on about bloody amateur detectives. He explained that they had discovered Posh Ron's true identity through old dental and medical records. But he had to admit that they hadn't made the connection between Posh Ron and Terry. Nick asked if they had caught him yet, he replied it was only a matter of time. Nick then asked him why he had arrested Angus. He replied that they were acting on information received.

'You've been talking to Kate, haven't you,' Nick said.

'She said that she had seen him lurking around the churchyard just before the body was discovered.'

'He most probably nipped out for a cigarette, as the door to his office is only ten yards away,' Nick said, shaking his head.

'How was I to know that?' he said as his face was turning a very bright shade of red.

'And what about Rodney? I heard you gave him a hard time.'

'Ah, that was different, he lied to us.' His face was returning to its original colour.

'Go on,' Nick urged.

'Apparently, he was feeling a bit guilty about not bringing in any money on the account of being out of work. So, he had taken up gambling and he didn't want his partner to find out. As it happened, that day he had a win and he was going to collect his winnings, Two hundred quid. She forgave him but he had to promise not to gamble again and spend more time looking for a job.'

On Sunday, Howard South, Nick's union representative appeared. They went over his statement, and he filled Nick in on recent developments. Apparently, the class in question was attending a tutorial session in the afternoon following the incident. Their tutor, Mary Oswald, overheard them talking and questioned them. She reported her findings to the 'turd' Mark Robertson, who in turn made them write statements to the effect that Nick swore and threatened them. These statements were presented to the Vice Principal and so the enquiry started. The rumourmongers at the college insisted that Mark and Mary were having an affair, which would explain a lot. Because all the students involved would have to be interviewed, with their parents, separately, no date for the hearing has been made.

Nick was discharged on Monday morning. He phoned his best friend Don Patrick, who had been visiting his in-laws in Devon for the past week to collect him. He drove Nick home in his new BMW and gave him a bottle of Laphroaig to help him recover.

Tuesday 24 February 2004

Nick was feeling a lot better on Tuesday; he showered, shaved then watched his favourite Harry Potter film, *The Prisoner of Azkaban* on DVD. It was now 12.00 noon, and he was feeling a little hungry. Maybe, he thought, he'll pop along to the pub for some lunch. He parked his bike in the Mermaid and walked to the High Street. He needed some cash and the nearest hole in the wall was at the Barclays Bank. Nick was lost in his thoughts but still aware of his surroundings. Then Nick saw him on the other side of the road, the turd, Mark Robertson. He was about fifty yards away walking in Nick's direction. He looked around, not much traffic about, so he crossed the road. Up to this point he still didn't know if the turd actually knew him. As he walked towards Nick, he gave no indication that this was so. The path was standard size with a three-foot-high wall on one side. Nick kept near the kerb so that he would have to pass between him and the wall. As he approached, Nick gradually narrowed the gap so there was just enough space for him to pass. A quick glance around told him that there was no one close by. What would Reacher say, 'make it quick', no witnesses, and no marks. As he squeezed between Nick and the wall, he hit him in the Solar Plexus. Nick carried on walking. Don't look back; Nick heard a voice in my head say. But he couldn't resist a quick look; he was on his knees gasping for breath. Nick smiled; yes, that did feel good.

Nick bought a newspaper on the way back to the pub and was now enjoying his pint and looking at the headlines on the front page:

LORD LUCAN MURDERED
KILLER DISAPPEARS

The Scottish Ale

From the bonny bells of heather
They brewed a drink long-syne,
Was sweeter far from honey,
Was stronger far than wine.
They brewed it and they drank it
And lay in a blessed swound
For days and days together
In their dwellings underground.
Marian McNeil, 1956

The Scottish Ale

PROLOGUE

Back in Scotland and demoralized, many of Charles' men returned to their homes, and the Government army, now led by the King's son the Duke of Cumberland, caught up with the Jacobite forces at Culloden on 16 April 1746. Charles' forces, by now hungry and exhausted, were massacred. Cumberland ordered his men to give no quarter to their opponents, and for the merciless treatment given to wounded and fleeing men, he is still referred to in the Highlands as Butcher Cumberland.

Charles himself escaped from the battlefield and his subsequent flight around the Highlands and Islands, pursued by Government troops and aided by many Highlanders despite the huge price on his head has become the stuff of many legends. It was his flight through the Isle of Skye, however, aided by Flora MacDonald, which is best remembered.

Flora was born on South Uist though she was raised at Armadale in Sleat. In 1746 she was living in Benbecula when the fleeing Prince arrived, seeking refuge and a safe hiding place. She disguised the prince as her maid Betty Burke, and they were rowed across the Minch with a crew of six, landing at what is now known as Prince Charles' Point in Trotternish, a couple of miles north of Uig.

They hid there in a cottage before making a clandestine overland journey to Portree together. They stayed overnight in an Inn, now known as 'The Isle Inn', before they parted. Charles gave Flora a locket with his portrait and promised they would meet again. Charles hid for a time on Raasay but his flight continued with a gruelling march from Portee to Egol, undertaken by night. They crossed the moors to Sligachan before passing over the Red Hills just north of Marsco before going on to through the Strath Mor and eventually reaching Egol where Charles stayed overnight in a cave before taking another boat for the mainland. He eventually made it back to France, sailing from Arisaig on 20 September.

May 2004

It is a warm Thursday evening late May and Nick Allen has just returned home after an exciting cricket match in which his team *Garden Fields Parents CC* (also known as Men of Fields) has just defeated *Manland School Parents CC* by seven runs. As always, they take great delight in beating any team from Harpenden, especially *Manland.* Nick's team is under the impression that all men from Harpenden are in-bred, have no chins, and are called Julian. Tonight's victory is even more impressive because Nick's side batted first and after the allotted twenty overs, had scored a less than impressive 86 runs. At this level in a Twenty20 match one would expect a score in the region of 120 runs. In normal circumstances one would be thinking of an early bath, but as there are no changing facilities in the middle of Verulamium Park, then it would be an early beer. But *Garden Fields CC* is no ordinary team. For them. a mixture of players, gentlemen, and good chaps, losing is not an option. Cricket is not Nick's main sport, but he's always available, can hit a few runs and turn his arm when necessary. But he does stand out in one particular field; he is the team's motivator. It was his late wife Jane's idea; after driving pass a cricket match in Chislehurst, she saw one team in a huddle and suggested that he should do the same thing. So, at some point in their matches they have, what is now known affectionately as 'Ol' Nicks huddle'. It does seem amazing, but they have never lost a match after a huddle. But tonight, they would need something really special if were to rescue this match. Nick liked to vary the huddles, sometimes a raucous chant or a witty poem but luckily, he had something special planned for tonight's game.

They assembled on the edge of the square and formed the usual circle. Nick lit a joss stick and stuck it the ground. Then he took the match ball out of his pocket and said, 'I call to the spirit of St Alban to bless this ball, may it stick in our hands and never cross the boundary,' He then kissed the ball and said, 'bless this ball'. Then passing the ball to his left and each player in turn kissed and blessed the ball. They then bowled *Manland* all out for 79 runs. It was a game to remember, and the London Pride flowed as they celebrated their win with the usual sausage and chips at the *Six Bells* public house.

It's been a year now since Nick's wife Jane passed away and things haven't been easy. He was recently suspended from his position as a lecturer in mathematics at the St Albans Regional College. After a farcical disciplinary hearing he was found guilty of threatening behaviour towards students, but the charge of Gross Misconduct was reduced to Serious Misconduct, and he was given a final warning. Tomorrow is the last day before half-term. He has survived the last six weeks; they have taken the offending class in question off his timetable and things seem to be improving.

Next Day
'Not on holiday again?' remarked Rodney Black, a close friend of Nick's.

He's relaxing with friends in the beer garden of the Mermaid Public House; it is Friday, early evening.

'I wouldn't call it a holiday, more like convalescence,' he replied.

'Aye laddie, it has only been six weeks since yer last break' snarled Angus Gold, another friend of Nick's. 'Yer must be exhausted.'

'Leave him alone,' interrupted Diana, an attractive sixty-year-old sitting at the next table. 'He's had a hard time recently,'

'Thank you, Di,' replied Nick, smiling across to her. 'It's nice to see that someone cares.'

'My pleasure'.'

'So, Nick back to the question in hand,' stated Mick, a quiet man in his forties, 'what is your favourite all time joke?'

'Let me think,' stroking his chin as if in deep thought, 'ah yes. A young American walks into the office of a famous talent agent. He says, 'I've come for an interview; I can sing, dance, act and tell jokes.'

'Okay,' replied the talent agent, 'show me what you can do.'

After going through a twenty-minute routine the agent says 'kid, you're great, I'll sign you up straight away. In six months, you'll have your own TV series and I'll get you in films, maybe even on Broadway.'

'That's great, thank you.'

'No problem, I'll just get a contract for you to sign. Now what's your name?'

'Penis Van Lesbian.'

'What?'

'Penis Van Lesbian.'

'You can't have a name like that; you'll have to change it'.

'I can't change it, it's my family name. I'll go to another agency if I must'.

'Fine; but no one will hire you with that name.'

'We'll see.'

'If you change your mind the offer's still open.'

With that he walked out of the door.

Three months later he reappeared.

'You were right, no one with hire me, so I've done as you suggested, I've changed my name'.

'That's great kid, so what have you called yourself?'

'Dick Van Dyke.'

'That's awful,' groaned Rodney.

'No, it's clever,' Nick replied.

Just then they were interrupted by Ken the landlord. He was carrying a tray full of half pint glasses of beer. Ken, in his early thirties, always wears jeans and a brewery t-shirt and brews his own beer at a local brewery.

'I want you to try this new beer I've brewed. I'm thinking of entering it for the St Albans Beer festival, and I think it's a winner.'

He placed the tray on the table, and they all took a glass.

'What do you think?' he asked expectantly.

'It's okay,' replied Mick.

'Quite nice.' admitted Rodney.

'Not quite my thing laddie, but it seems okay.' was Angus's reply.

'Nick, what do you think,' Ken asked despondently.

'It's too hoppy for my taste; you know I prefer malty beers.'

Looking disappointed Ken says, 'I really need to win a prize this year; I need to get my beers on the map.'

'Maybe I can help ye laddie. I have a secret recipe for a Scottish beer. Been handed down from generation to generation, it's a real winner.' Angus gave a sly smile. 'Leave it with me, I'll dig it out.'

'Thanks a lot Angus,' smiled Ken. 'But bring it in soon, we'll need to try it and time's running out'.

Ken retreated to the bar, and they all looked at Angus.

'What?' he said looking as if butter wouldn't melt in his mouth.

'Since when have you had secret recipes for Scottish beer, lager boy?' Nick said mockingly.

'I canna say where it comes from but mark my words it's a winner.'

'Well, you better not let him down, it means a lot to him.' piped in Rodney.

'Aye, ye can trust me laddie.'

The evening continued with light-hearted banter; they were joined by Blind Bill. Bill, mid-fifties, who was blinded following a car crash thirty years ago. He was accompanied by his guide dog, Cadbury, a chocolate Labrador. Nick always carried a few dog chews in his pocket, and he always looks him out when he's in the pub. Nick spent a few minutes making a fuss of him. He remembered once that Cadbury got so excited seeing him that he pulled Bill off his stool. Next. to join them. was Annie Castle, a colleague of Nick's from the college; she was head of the Art department. Annie was about fifty, slim, attractive, and very arty with a good sense of humour. She was accompanied by a lady Nick hadn't seen before. She was introduced as Mary McGregor, who would be joining the college next term. Mary, Nick guessed would be about forty, jet black hair, very pale skin, and reminded him of Snow White. She spoke with a broad Scottish accent. This would please Angus he thought; and was right!

'Let me find yer a seat lassie and come and join us. It will make a change to have some decent conversation.'

Angus and Mary hit it off straight away. It was nice to see Angus with a woman. In all the years Nick had known him, he didn't think he has ever had a girlfriend. *Will I ever find love again; it's been a year since my Jane died? Not yet, its way to soon, I'm still grieving,* thought Nick.

Wednesday, the following week

Nick spent the half term week relaxing, catching up with old friends, gardening, and the like. On Wednesday Nick met his daughter Sarah for lunch, who works in London as a Chartered Accountant, and they spent a pleasant hour in the *All Bar One* where he enjoyed a steak sandwich and a glass of Leffe. After that he decided to visit a couple of interesting pubs. First was the *Cittie of Yorke* in High Holborn. This *Samuel Smith's* pub is like no other. You enter a mighty 'olde Englishe' hall with a high roof, massive wine vats and a high-level window where the lord of the manor might once have presided over the proceedings. He enjoyed a pint of *Samuel Smith's Old Brewery Bitter* and at 4.0% it has a good head, fruity aroma, and very nice bitter taste. His next stop was the *Jerusalem Tavern* in Clerkenwell; this fantastic little pub is a recent re-creation, bought and restored by St. Peter's Brewery, Suffolk. Formerly it was a town house built in 1720, it was converted into a watchmaker's shop a hundred years later and a shop front was added. It became a pub in 1996, but the job has been done so well it's hard to believe it's not original. All the Real Ales are served straight from the casks which are mounted on the wall, Nick went for the Organic Best Bitter at 4.1%. This pale bronze beer has a biscuity malt and peppery hops aroma, followed by an explosion of spicy, bitter hop resins on the tongue with a good balance of sappy malt and tart fruit. As it was mid-afternoon the pub was relatively quiet, and he spent a pleasant hour talking to the attractive Irish barmaid about interesting London pubs. The pub is just a few minutes' walk from Farringdon station, so the journey home was quick and uneventful.

One evening in July.

Angus was true to his word and produced a recipe for a Scottish Ale. It consisted of roast barley, rolled Scottish oatmeal and Scottish heather honey. He used his connections back in Scotland to supply the ingredients at a reasonable cost. So, for the next few weeks Angus and Ken were busy trying out different proportions of the ingredients until they were satisfied that they had found the perfect blend. Nick had never seen Ken looking so happy and Angus had an extra spring in his step. Could there be romance in the air.

It takes about three weeks to brew a beer from scratch, and they tried a few variations of the quantities, but in the end settled for the original recipe. When the brew was finally ready Ken organized a special tasting evening. He invited all the regulars, put on a small buffet and we waited in anticipation. Nick was sitting at a table with Angus, Rodney, Mary and Annie. They were not disappointed; it was delicious, smooth, and distinctively dark with a Stout-like bitterness and an ABV of 4.5%. Ken was ecstatic and he kept refilling our glasses and making toasts to Angus, Mary, and everyone else there.

'So, Angus,' Nick slurred 'what is the secret of your recipe?'

'Aye laddie,' he replied. 'I wondered when ye were gonna ask me that. Well, I'm gonna tell yer, but it must be kept a secret. There are people out there that would kill to get their hands on this recipe.'

They all tried not to laugh but promised and moved closer to hear his tale.

'It goes back to 1746.'

'It always does,' said Nick.

'Bonnie Prince Charlie was on the run from those dammed English. With the help of Flora Macdonald, he managed to get to the Isle of Skye. They made their way to Portree where they stayed in an Inn overnight. Charlie was exhausted so the landlady Janet Cornfoot gave him a pint of beer. He was so impressed by it, that he asked her for the recipe, stating that when he became King, he would give this beer to all his troops on his coronation day. So, she copied the recipe out on a piece of parchment; on the back she wrote '*To Charlie, our one true Prince. May the force be with you*' and signed it, *Janet Cornfoot.* Don't you see that this parchment is worth a fortune; it should really be in a museum. It is an actual piece of history.'

'So how come you have it, Angus?' asked Rodney, not totally convinced.

'Well, when Charlie and Flora left the Inn the next morning, they parted and went they separate ways. Charlie gave Flora the parchment for safe keeping. Anyway, one of my distant relatives was a minister in Trotternish and she told him the story on her death bed and gave him the parchment for safe keeping and it has been in the family ever since.'

'Well,' said Nick, 'true or not it's a bloody good story and Angus is pretty clued up on his Scottish history.' Mary stood up and said she had a headache and was going home. Angus offered to phone for a taxi, but she said no, the walk might help. She pecked him on the cheek and said goodbye to the rest of us.

I might be half cut, but that was a strange look that Mary gave Angus as she walked out of the door, thought Nick.

'May the force be with you? You're having a laugh Angus,' said Rodney.

'No laddie, what I didn't tell ye, that Janet was a witch, and she practiced the old ways. It is a common term in pagan talk. That's where they got it from. Look it up if ye don't believe me'.

At this point Kate, our local alcoholic staggered past.

'How's it going boys?' she slurred, 'having a nice evening?

'Fine thanks,' said Nick, 'what's new with you?'

'Just booked a weekend in Rome,' she replied, 'gonna take in a bit of culture.'

'That's nice,' replied Nick trying to look interested. How she manages to stay upright on those high heels I'll never know.

'Did you know that Michelangelo painted sixteen chapels?'

'Amazing' he said, as she disappeared into the Ladies toilet. The evening is getting stranger by the minute. Then Ken appeared, grinning like a Cheshire cat.

'I've had a brilliant idea.' he exclaimed, 'listen; I'm going to hire a Dray and a horse to pull it. I'm going to dress up in Highland gear, you know, kilt, sporran, all the gear and I'll be a Highland Laird or whatever they call them. And Angus, well you've got the outfit already, you can lead the Dray playing the bagpipes and Annie and Mary can accompany me on the Dray. I'll get costumes for you too and, I Nick and Rodney can walk behind, like a guard. I'll get costumes for you as well. It'll be great and we can take the beer to the festival. We'll start at the pub then go down the St. Peters Street and back then to the Arena. Think how much publicity it will generate; everyone will want to taste it....but we haven't got a name...we've got to have a name'.

'Calm down,' said Annie. 'We can soon think of a name. What about *Angus Gold*? After all it was his recipe'

'But it's not a Golden Ale, look at it, it's almost Black,' Nick informed her.

'That's it,' shouted Ken, 'we'll call it ***Black Angus***. '

The St Albans Beer Festival is held over 4 days at the end of September at the St Albans Arena. Two beers from each of the seven breweries in Hertfordshire are put forward for the 'Hertfordshire Beer of the Year'. These beers are chosen by the Brewery Liaison Officer nominated by CAMRA (Campaign for Real Ale). Ken has good connections with CAMRA, so getting ***Black Angus*** nominated shouldn't be a problem. The beers are delivered on the Monday and the tasting for the 'Best Beer' takes place on the first day (Wednesday). A new rule was introduced this year that all the beers being judged must be in place by 2:00pm on the Monday.

It was agreed that the Dray should arrive at 1:00pm which would give them enough time to parade down the St. Peters Street before delivering the beer. The costumes would be delivered in the morning, and they would meet at 11.00am which would give them enough time to get ready. Annie and Nick both stated that they would throw a sickie that day. Angus would take a day's holiday; Rodney is still looking for work and Mary was free that day.

Late September, two's day before the festival

Nick arrived on time for the big day; Rodney and Annie were already there. There was no sign of Angus or Mary. The pub was still closed; the costumes were left on the doorstep. There was no sign of Ken or June, her shift started at 11.00am.

'How's Angus getting here?' Nick asked Rodney.

'Taxi,' he replied.

'Give him a ring Rodney, see where he is.'

'No reply.'

'What taxi firm does he use?'

'The usual one.'

'Well give them a ring; see if they know anything.'

They waited a few moments.

'They haven't heard from him today.'

Nick was getting worried. 'I don't like this, and where the hell is Ken?'

'Do you think something has happened?' enquired Annie.

'I'm not sure, but I've got a horrible feeling about this.'

'I think we should do something,' said Annie.

'Okay this is what we'll do, Rodney, you come with me, Annie you stay here and wait for June. Ring me if you find Ken but we'll get back as soon as possible.'

Nick and Rodney jumped into the car and fled towards Angus's bungalow. It wasn't far and they were there in a couple of minutes. Nick drove slowly past the bungalow and noticed a large blue Volvo parked on the drive. It had a Scottish sticker on the back window. He parked the car about 20 yards further down, they got out and walked casually back to the bungalow. They walked past slowly and discreetly observed the frontage. The curtains were drawn in the living room which would make their approach unobserved. Quietly they crept to the bungalow, Nick noticed a small gap in the curtains, just enough to survey the situation. He didn't like what he saw. Angus was tied to a chair; he was naked except for a sporran covering his manhood. Standing above him was a large, bearded man in a kilt brandishing a large sword. He looked like the actor *Brian Blessed.* Nick summoned Rodney to have a look. He started laughing, so Nick clipped him round the head and dragged him back to the car.

'Listen,' Nick said. 'I want you to phone the police and wait here for them.'

'What are you going to do?' he replied in a worried voice.

'I'm going to rescue Angus.'

'Don't be silly Nick, that bloke has got a sword.'

'Angus is in danger,' replied Nick, as he took his golfing umbrella out of the boot. 'A man's gotta do what a man's gotta do.'

Nick quietly ran down the drive and found a side door that led to the kitchen. He was in luck as the door was not locked. He carefully opened the door and crept in. So far so good but what to do now? *I've got my umbrella, but would that be enough?* He looked around and found a block of kitchen knives, pulled one out and slid it in his trouser belt towards his back so it couldn't be seen. There was another door that led to the hall, and it was open. From the door to the hall, Nick could see the door that led to the living room, it was ajar. *Here goes,* he thought. He kicked the door open and walked in, umbrella at the ready.

'Well, well, what have we here?' said the bearded man in the kilt. 'Planning a little rescue, are we?'

Nick looked over to Angus; he has a large red mark around his eye and small cuts all over his body. He was looking very worried.

'Well, that's the general plan,' he replied with a smirk on his face.

He laughed. 'How typical, an Englishman with an umbrella, I'm surprised you're not wearing a bowler hat. Who do you think you are *John Steed?'*

'The names Allen, Nick Allen and I'm not afraid of some bearded lady in a skirt; so, tell me before I whip your arse, who are you and what do you want?'

'Okay,' he replied, 'before I cut you in two, I'll tell you. My name is Rory and I belong to an ancient Scottish order called the *Beggars Bennison.* We are the keepers of all the artifacts relating to the Jacobite Revolution, and our friend here has something that doesn't belong to him.'

Nick laughed, 'you mean the recipe, that's not real; he made that story up. God almighty, you are as thick as you look.'

Nick thought that was one insult too many as Rory raised his sword and took a downward swipe. It's funny what you think at times like this, but Nick recognized his sword as a 'Basket-hilted Claymore' with a 35-inch blade. The attack was telegraphed, and he easily stepped aside. He stumbled a little and Nick gave him a good prod in the ribs with his umbrella. He was now really incensed and lunged with his Claymore. Even at 54 years old Nick's reflexes are finely tuned and he just managed to avoid the deadly blade. As it flew passed him, he pulled out the kitchen knife with his left hand and plunged it into his upper arm. He screamed, grabbed the knife handle, but before he could remove it, Nick dropped his umbrella and hit him with a right hook. It landed perfectly on the chin, and he was out cold before he hit the floor. Nick stood over him like a victorious gladiator when Angus screamed, 'look behind yer.'

Entering the room from another door was Mary. Her eyes were bulging, her hair was standing on end like she had been electrocuted and her teeth were bared. She was holding a Sgian Dubh (a black dagger). Then screaming like a banshee, she leapt at Nick; a straight right took care of her.

'Well done laddie, now come and untie me,' said Angus looking a little relieved.

As Nick approached him, they heard the sound of police cars pulling up outside.

'Sorry Angus, I've got to go, there's another person missing. Tell the police I'll give them a statement latter.'

As Nick left the bungalow, he met DS Blakely walking down the drive.

'And where do you think you are going?' he asked grabbing his arm.

'Sorry mate got to go, catch you later. It's all sorted in there, but you will need an ambulance.'

Nick pulled away from him, called to Rodney; they both jumped in the car and fled towards the Mermaid.

June had arrived, she had overslept; she had opened the pub but no sign of Ken.

'It looks like there has been a struggle,' said Jane as she started tidying the lounge 'but Ken is so untidy you can't tell the difference,'

'Let's keep looking, we might find a clue to his whereabouts.' Nick said in desperation.

'Look,' gasped June, 'there's a message on the answerphone. Shall I play it?'

'Of course,' Nick replied, 'it can't do any harm.'

A man's voice on the answerphone said 'Listen carefully; I shall say this only once. If you want to see your landlord again do not, I repeat, do not enter your Scottish Ale for the Beer Festival.'

Annie and Rodney had joined them, Rodney started to panic. 'What shall we do, what shall we do,' he screamed.

Nick clipped him round the head again and said, 'Listen, I think I recognize that voice, but we need to know where he is. I have an idea; I want us all to listen to the message again with our eyes shut. Try to cut out his voice and concentrate on the sounds in the background. We might be able to tell where he is phoning from.'

So, they all closed their eyes and played the tape back. After the third play Rodney said, 'There is a lot of activity and background noise but I'm sure I heard the sound of barrels being moved.'

'That's right.' exclaimed June. 'I bet he's calling from the festival.'

'But we still don't know who he is,' said Annie.

'It's a long shot,' I said, 'but try ringing 1471.'

June picked up the phone and dialled it then, smiling she said, 'we've got his mobile number.'

'Excellent,' Nick replied, 'I have a cunning plan. June, you stay here just in case. Rodney and Annie come with me.'

It was only a short walk to the Arena, and they managed to sneak in without any problem as there was lots of activity with all the brewers delivering their beers. They went upstairs to the balcony where they had a good view of all the people.

'Okay,' Nick said, looking a little concerned. 'Rodney, if you go about 10 yards to my right and Annie you go 10 yards to my left. I'll ring the number. Keep your eyes peeled for anyone answering a mobile. I try to keep him talking to give you more time.'

Nick dialled the number; it rang for a while before someone answered. He signalled to Rodney and Annie, and they started scrutinizing the crowd.

'Hello,' the voice said.

'Hi there,' Nick replied. 'Can I speak to Dean please?'

'I think you have the wrong number.'

'Sorry, what was that? I can't hear you very well. There is a lot of noise.'

'I said you have the wrong number.'

'What number is this?'

'You should know, you've just rung it,' he sounded irritated.

Nick looked to his left and saw Annie pointing to the crowd. Excellent he thought what a great girl Annie is.

'Sorry,' Nick said and hung up.

41

He ran over to Annie.

'Who is it?' he asked.

'That one there, the one with the beard; he's wearing a black t-shirt. He's talking to that woman in the red dress.'

'I know him,' Nick gasped. 'His name is Tony; he owns the Orchid Brewery. I've seen him in the Mermaid a few times recently.'

'Why would he kidnap Ken?' asked Ralph.

'It's obvious; he knows Ken's beer stands a better chance of winning than his.'

'So, what are we going to do?'

'We'll go back to the Mermaid and try to figure out where he is holding Ken'.

They scurried back to the pub, called June, and waited in the bar.

'We haven't got much time; the deadline is in two hours,' said June.

'It's a long shot, but I think they are holding him at their brewery,' Nick said.

'But where is their brewery?' asked Rodney.

'I'm not sure, but you can look it up on your fancy mobile.'

After a minute searching Rodney exclaimed 'Got it; the brewery is at Parsons Farm in a village called Henham, just outside Bishops Stortford'.

'Well done, Rodders, that's our next port of call. Okay, Rodders you come with me. Annie, you stay here with June, the dray will be here at 1.00pm. Even if we don't get back in time that beer is going to the festival. Annie, get changed just in case, I think you will look good in a kilt.'

Nick checked the directions on his map; Henham was about 30 miles away. If he took the A414 then pick up the A10 after that it's all B roads. It could take an hour to get there. He'll have to put his foot down. *What we need is some good music to help, some psychedelic pop should do.* He put *Restless Night* by *Octopus* into the CD player as they drove off to Henham. They were lucky, that the roads were clear, and they made it in 45 minutes. They found the farm quite easily, it looked deserted. The brewery was situated in a barn to the left of the farm. It was surrounded by a six-foot fence with a gate that was padlocked.

Nick told Rodney to stand by the car and he scaled over the fence. He could see two doors in front of him, one was padlocked the other looked like an outside toilet. They were about 30 yards away. He was about 20 yards from the padlocked door when suddenly, a large Alsatian dog appeared and ran towards him barking ferociously. Nick stood still, frozen to the spot. The dog stopped in front of him still barking. *What can I do* he thought, this dog is not going to let me move. Nick smiled, slowly slid his hand to the lower pocket in his chinos and pulled out six dog chews that he had saved for Cadbury. He threw one to the dog; he sniffed at it then ate it. Nick gave him another one; he quickly scoffed that one down to. The next one he threw towards the outside toilet; he ran after it and quickly consumed it. Then the next one landed right outside the toilet. Nick walked over to the toilet opened the door and threw the next dog chew inside. The dog followed it in; he shut the door behind it; job done. He then ran to the padlocked door, shouted out 'Ken'. To my relief he answered, 'In here'.

Nick looked round and found an engineering brick. Ideal he thought and used it to smash the lock. Ken was tied to a pillar that supported the roof, at least he is not naked Nick thought. He untied him and they ran back to the fence. Nick easily climbed over the fence; Ken struggled.

'You need to lose some weight if this is going to be a regular occurrence,' Nick joked.

'I'll leave the adventure stuff to you; I need a pint' he laughed as they scrambled back to the car. Nick checked his watch; it was now 1.00pm, only 1 hour before the deadline.

They headed back home; Nick put a different CD on. This time he selected *Odessey & Oracle* by *The Zombies,* his favourite band. Nick told Rodney to phone the Mermaid and tell them that they had found Ken. June replied saying that the Dray had just arrived and so had DS Blakley. While Rodney was on the mobile, Nick quickly formulated another cunning plan. Rodney passed his idea to DS Blakley just in case they didn't make it in time.

When they arrived back at the Mermaid the Dray was loaded, Annie looked cute in her Highland outfit, as did DS Blakey, who wasn't looking too amused. It was a very hot day and as well as sweating profusely the horse had a massive erection. Annie was looking a little embarrassed.

'Throw a bucket of water over that thing,' Nick shouted to June. 'Ken, Rodney and I need to get changed quickly'.

They were back down in five minutes; Ken got into position on the Dray accompanied by Annie and DS Blakley. Rodney and Nick walked behind as an escort. They went straight to the Arena, not having enough time to do the full tour. They unloaded the first barrel and put it onto the sack-barrow. There was a great round of applause as Ken accompanied by Annie and Rodney pushed the first barrel into the arena. DS Blakely and Nick went in search of the kidnapper Tony. Nick spotted him not far away and pointed him out to DS Blakley. Tony was looking decidedly uncomfortable as DS Blakley approached him.

'I'm arresting you on the suspicion of kidnapping and false imprisonment, anything you say will be….'

Before he had chance to finish reading him his rights, Tony pushed him in the chest and ran towards the exit. As he ran past Nick, he stuck out his foot and Tony went flying over it. As he landed on the floor two burly police officers appeared, handcuffed him, and took him away. Nick turned around to look for DS Blakey, he quickly appeared, gave him a high five as they disappeared to find the nearest bar.

The following Saturday

Ken's beer *'Black Angus'*, won the title of 'Hertfordshire Beer of the Year'. He arranged to hold a party to celebrate his award. Angus was released after an overnight stay in hospital after receiving a few stitches to the more serious cuts. Rory was now in custody after receiving treatment for a very serious knife wound. Mary was being held in the psychiatric ward of the local hospital nursing a very sore chin. It was a warm pleasant evening, so they all sat outside. Ken was hosting the party, Rodney, Angus, Annie, DS Blakley, and June (it was her night off), plus Mick, Blind Bill (without Cadbury), Colin, the pig farmer, Nick's best mate Don Patrick, Di and a few others all sat around drinking lashings of their favourite Scottish Ale.

'So,' Nick asked Angus, 'what happened to Mary?'

'Well laddie, I'll tell thee. As ye would have guessed, Mary was also a member of the *Beggar's Bennison,* and she informed the order about my recipe. After they had broken into the house and tied me up, they tortured me. I held out as long as I could, but Mary said she would castrate me if I didn't tell them. So, I told them where the recipe was. She was in the bedroom retrieving it when Nick turned up.'

'You mean it actually exists?'

'Of course, it does, you doubting Sassenach. But what I didn't tell them was that it comes with a curse. Anyone who tries to steal it from its rightful heir is visited by a ghost.'

'That's why Mary was shouting 'keep the witch away,' when she came round,' interrupted DS Blakely. 'And she claims the witch is still with her. That's why she's locked away in a padded cell.'

'Do you miss her?' asked Annie, 'I know she was very fond of you.'

'Well, she obviously had good taste in men,' he smirked. 'But I think I'm doomed to be single. She was a lovely lass, but there's too much heartache in falling in love, I'll stick with *Stella.*'

Nick stood up, 'I propose a toast, 'Ken and **Black Angus.**'

The gang all stood up raised their glasses and shouted, 'Ken and **Black Angus,**'

Then Angus shouted, 'I propose a toast to Janet Cornfoot.'

Before anyone could respond all the lights started to flicker, a cold wind blew through them, and a sound of ghostly laughter was heard.

They all laughed, raised their glasses and shouted, 'Janet Cornfoot.'

EPILOGUE

The Beggars Bennison was formed in 1732; it consisted of the most influential men in 18th century Scotland. They met twice a year in secret in a ruined castle and had two things on their minds. One was treason, the other the measurement of their penises. It is said that they wore ceremonial robes, and the Sovereign of the order wore a large wig made from the pubic hair of Charles II's mistresses. They had elaborate rituals, which included the measurement of their members on a specially

45

commissioned pewter plate. When the treasonable politics and the measuring was over, they got stuck into supper, after which they would listen to a paper on some aspect of sex – as on St Andrews Day in 1733, when they listened to a lecture on menstruation in skate.

For all this time some local girl, paid sums ranging from five shillings to a pound, lolled stark naked in a chair, her face covered, with no member of the order allowed to touch her.

The Order had their own Bible, an anthology, with illustrations, of the most prurient passages, decorated with the coats of arms of the Scottish nobility who belonged (from the Duke of Gordon to the Earl of Lauderdale). Even George IV belonged, and when one of the members made off with the wig, the King graciously presented them with a silver snuffbox containing the pubic hair of his current mistress, thus preserving, albeit in a minor mode, the Royal connection.

The Pig Farmer

"Maybe love at first sight isn't what we think, maybe it's recognising a soul we loved in a past life and falling in love with them again."

This story contains some adult themes.

The Pig Farmer

1643

Throughout the English Civil Wars, St. Albans was a Parliamentary stronghold. A Parliamentary garrison was stationed at St. Albans from 1442 onwards. The town was put into a permanent state of defence. In fact, St. Albans was a crucial strategic importance to Parliament as commanders ranging from Earl of Essex to Sir Thomas Fairfax used it as their headquarters.

It is a fine October morning as Sir Nicholas Capel look out over his estate at Gorhambury. The harvest was good, and all things should be well, but there is trouble in the air. A Civil War has just started and many of the influential men in St Albans, as well as the rest of Hertfordshire had decided before the outbreak of war to side with the Parliamentarians rather than King Charles. Despite the County's declared allegiance, there were still many, including Sir Nicholas who are prominent Royalists.

'My Lord, my Lord.' It was his faithful manservant, Ralph; a small 16-year-old ginger-haired boy, whom he had rescued in Ireland whilst visiting his good friend Sir Patrick three years ago. He was at the time being beaten up by a gang of ruffians who had accused him of stealing eggs from their farm. Sir Nicholas saw them off with his trusty blade, brought him back to England and he has been in his service ever since.

'What is it, Ralph?' Sir Nicholas asked.

'Parliamentarians,' he gasped 'they are approaching the house.'

'I had feared this might happen,' he replied. 'You had better bring me my trusty sword.'

'Right away, sweet master.'

He returned within a minute; Sir Nicholas strapped on his sword.

'Where is my wife, Lady Jane?' he enquired.

'She is in the kitchen helping prepare tonight's meal.'

'Please inform her of the situation, and tell her code red.'

'Yes, sweet master.'

'And where is my daughter, the fair Lady Sarah?'

'I believe she is in the stables.'

'Please inform her also.'

'It's as good as done, sweet master.'

With that he disappeared. Sir Nicholas stepped out of the main door just as ten Parliamentarians rode up and dismounted. He addressed the one he believed to be the leader. 'Pray what can I do for you soldier?'

'We need refreshment, and our horses need watering,' the leader replied.

'There are barracks in St Albans which will give you what you need, why have you made this detour?'

'Maybe there are things here that are not available at St Albans,' he laughed.

The other Parliamentarians also laughed.

'I do not like your tone of voice; I think you should leave now while you are still able to ride.'

Sir Nicholas withdrew his sword.

They laughed again.

'One against ten, the odds do not favour you Sir Nicholas.'

'Two against ten,' says a voice to the right.

They looked round and saw Lady Jane. She was wearing a pair of brown riding trousers with a bright green bodice which showed off her magnificent bosom. That outfit always makes Sir Nicholas's blood rise. I shall certainly ravage her tonight, he thought.

'Three against ten,' another voice came from his left.

It was their daughter, Lady Sarah standing there. Sixteen years old, despite dressed as a stable lad, her blond hair shone in the late afternoon sun. Her blue eyes sparkled as did the sword she is holding. They both smiled; their daughter is an accomplished swordswoman.

When the odds are stacked against you, first identify the leader, take him out, and then go for the next two in the chain of command. Sir Nicholas went for the leader whilst Jane and Sarah picked their opponents. It wasn't much of a contest; Sir Nicholas quickly disarmed the leader whilst Jane and Sarah battled quite comfortably with two opponents each. Now Ralph,

*despite numerous lessons is the worst swordsman on the planet.
But he has the heart of a lion and very nibble and has a knack of
appearing from nowhere and clouting the opposition on the head
with a large wooden club. Within a few minutes three of the
soldiers were unconscious, thanks to Ralph. The girls' opponents
were on the ground nursing various sword wounds, whilst the
other two didn't fancy a fight and were last seen galloping
towards St Albans.*

*'Now,' says Sir Nicholas addressing the leader who was
sitting on the ground looking up at the tip of my sword. 'You are
not welcome here, so be on your way.'*

'You haven't heard the last of this,' he scowled.

*They threw the unconscious soldiers onto their horses and the
leader led his defeated comrades away from the house.*

*That evening they enjoyed a hearty meal of Shoulder of
Mutton with Oysters washed down with homemade Mead. As
they laughed and raised a glass to King Charles, Lady Sarah,
noticed two weevils on the bread plate.*

*'Daddy dearest,' she says, 'if you had to choose between
those two weevils, which one would you choose?'*

*'An interesting question dear Sarah. They both look similar,
they seem to be the same length, but I think the one nearer the
edge of the plate is slightly fatter. I would choose that one.'*

*'Tut, tut dearest father didn't you always teach us to choose
the lesser of two weevils.'*

*Oh, how they laughed, if only life could be like this always.
They were then interrupted by a strange ringing sound.*

'Ralph,' Sir Nicholas shouted, what is that noise?'

'It's the phone, sweet master.'

But we don't have phones in 1643 he thought.

2004

Nick Allen woke up with a start; who's ringing me at this time
in the morning, he thought. It was his daughter Sarah.

'Hi dad, still in bed?' she asked.

'What time is it? he enquired .

'It's eight o'clock; I'm just on my way to the gym.'

'That's nice,' he replied, 'what else are you doing today?

51

'Having my hair done in London, and then going to Twickenham for the rugby; probably have a meal in Richmond afterwards; what are you doing?'

'The usual,' he replied.

'It's been over a year now since mum died, you need to move on. You are still a very attractive man you could find someone else.'

'No, it's still too soon; don't worry I'll be alright. So…' he replied, trying to change the subject, 'what have you got on at work next week?'

'Having dinner with Elton's manager on Monday, on Tuesday, at the Apple studios; do you need any more Beatles CD's?"

'Just the White Album, if you can manage that and maybe a few T-shirts.'

'I'll see what I can do. Oh, and Thursday I'm off to New York. Got to check on Paul McCartney's office; to see how they are doing after the divorce.'

'Who said a chartered accountant's life was boring?'

'Not me dad, got to go now, ring you tomorrow; bye.'

'Bye angel.'

What a strange dream he thought, I wonder if it means anything. He dismissed it, got out of bed, showered, and prepared for the weekend.

After completing his ablutions, he made breakfast and read the newspapers. At about noon he was walking around the market, which was what he did most Saturdays. First a visit to the bank, then to WHSmith for his lottery tickets, followed by Boots for toiletries. Visit a few stalls for his fruit and veg, occasionally, the pet stall for treats for Blind Bill's guide dog Cadbury. He always finishes off at the flower stall. He had been using this stall for forty years and he always bought his mum flowers from this stall until she died suddenly, she was 43 years old. Since he was married, he bought flowers for his wife Jane on a Saturday. He'd got very friendly with the stall holder, John. Nice man, about the same age. He hadn't told him that his wife has died and he always says, 'your wife will like these'. He always gave him a good deal.

He arrived at his local, the Mermaid, about 1:30pm. His friend Colin (the pig farmer) was already propping up the bar accompanied by a pint of cider.

'Hi Nick,' he says. 'Glad you have turned up, getting a bit lonely. What do you want?'

'Thanks, I'll have a pint of *Black Angus*,' Nick replied.

They were served by Ken the landlord. Ken had recently won *Hertfordshire Best Beer* with *Black Angus* at a recent Beer Festival.

'I need a word with you later,' says Ken, 'when it gets a bit quieter.'

'No problem,' Nick replied.

'What's that about,' asked Colin.

'No idea, but I bet he wants something. Anyway, how are you, you look a bit down.'

'How long have you got? he asked.

'All the time in the world, so fire away.'

'It's my wife Elizabeth, she's gone…. well, a bit funny.'

'Explain.'

'She won't come near me, sleeps in the spare room and cries a lot.'

'Menopause?'

'That's what I thought at first, but I don't think it is. She keeps saying that she has betrayed me. I asked her if there was another bloke and she screamed 'don't be stupid'. So, I asked her again what she meant, and she said she didn't know. This morning, she was crying again and saying that I was going to die, and it was all her fault.'

'She needs to see a doctor.'

'You're right; I'll make an appointment on Monday.'

'Try and get an emergency one, you need to sort this out as soon as.'

At this point Ken approached them.

'Got a minute? He asked.

Colin looked at Nick and said, 'that's okay.'

'Right Ken, fire away,' added Nick.

Ken was getting excited.

'We are hosting a St Albans Pub Quiz competition. Six pubs, including ours, will slug it out for the title of St Albans Pub Quiz Champions.'

'And?'

And I want you to get a team together to represent the Mermaid.'

'Okay.'

'What? You'll do it, no questions asked, no conditions.'

'What else have I got to do; we haven't had a murder or kidnapping in here for weeks now.'

'That's brilliant. I know you won't let me down. But there is one condition......you must have at least one female in the team.'

At that moment Kate, the local alcoholic, walked past.

'Who wants a female,' she asked.'

'It's for the pub's quiz team,' says Ken opening his mouth before engaging his brain.

Both Colin and Nick gave him a filthy look.

'Yeah, count me in, I'm good at quizzes.'

Ken looked at them and mouthed, 'sorry,' he said quickly 'so who else will be in your team, you need six.'

'Colin', Nick says, 'are you up to it?'

'Count me in,'

'Great, okay.... I know. Rodney, Angus, and my best mate Don. That should give us a good variety.'

'Are we going to have practice nights,' Kate asked, wobbling slightly on her high heels.

'Yes, we might have a practice night, but only if you stay sober,' says Nick sternly.

Kate was true to her word and according to Ken, when Nick popped in after work on Wednesday, he told him she had been sitting in the pub every afternoon this week reading the newspapers and trawling through quiz books. He also mentioned that whenever he wasn't serving, she was asking him to ask her a question.

'She's pretty hot on popular literature and pop music.'

'Well, that's good,' Nick replied, 'and you say she hasn't touched a drop.'

54

'Nothing stronger than orange juice; this could be the beginning of her recovery.'

'You could be right; she just needs something to focus on. Another soul saved.'

'Let's hope'.

At that point Colin walked in.

'Pint of Cider please Ken,'

'How did it go with Elizabeth at the doctors?' Nick asked.

'He's not sure; he thinks it's something psychological, given her some pills. Actually, she's getting worse; I heard her talking to herself the other day. She was talking with a strange accent, like old English and moaning about Oliver Cromwell. It really freaked me out.'

'Still in the spare room then?'

'Afraid so.'

Whether or not it was because he was thinking about Colin's problem, Nick didn't sleep well that night; but when he eventually dropped off the dream came back.

1643

Sir Nicholas is drinking in the Blue Boar public house in the Marketplace; it's renowned for its home-made brew. He's particularly partial to a pint of Cock Ale; the brewer always uses a fresh bird and quality French wine. He's accompanied by a good friend of his Sir Angus McGold, they are discussing business. He was just about to order another round when Ralph, his manservant came rushing in.

'Master, master,' he cried, 'I think there is going to be trouble outside.'

'What's happening?' Sir Nicholas asked.

'The High sheriff of Hertfordshire, Sir Thomas Coningsbury, with some others, are reading a proclamation on the steps of the Eleanor Cross.' It's from King Charles offering an amnesty to all who would no longer fight against him.'

'That's good, so what's the problem?'

'Cromwell and his troops are just down the road.'

'Shit!'

They rushed outside, but it was too late, Cromwell had arrived, and Sir Thomas was being manhandled away by the roundheads. Sir Nicholas went to draw his sword, but Sir Angus stopped him.

'Today is not a good day to die laddie, put ye sword away and we'll live to fight another day.'

The last they heard of him that he was taken to the Tower of London. Once order had been restored Ralph and Sir Nicholas rode back to Gorhambury with heavy hearts. They were greeted by Lady Sarah, who informed them that Sir Nicholas's sister-in-law had come to visit. Her name was Ellenor, and she was married to Sir Thomas Fairfax, the Commander of Parliament's New Model Army. Not a pleasant man and not one to tangle with. Ellenor was fair skinned, blonde hair and an all-woman figure. She and her sister Lady Jane are devoted to each other. Supper was being served as he entered the dining room. They were having a particular favourite of Sir Nicholas's, Potage of Venison followed by apple pie.

'Why is that bell ringing Ralph?' shouted Sir Nicholas.

'It's your alarm, sweet master.'

Bollocks, he thought.

2004

On Thursday evenings Nick always go out with his best mate, Don Patrick. They visit a few pubs, try some new beers and put the world to right. They had heard there was a new band on at the Farmers Boy, so they decided to check it out. Timothy Taylor's Landlord is their choice of beer this evening; at 4.3% it won't give them a headache in the morning. Apparently, it's Madonna favourite beer. The band performing tonight is called 'Elephant Shelf' and the lead singer and guitarist is a transvestite. He is joined by a female singer (They think she is a woman) who is an excellent singer but doesn't look comfortable performing. The band has a good following, but their own songs are a bit to repetitive. Nick and Don only stayed for one. They left the Farmers Boy and made their way to the White Lion and ordered two pints of Black Sheep. They sat down and Nick told Don about the dreams he was having and Colin's problems with Elizabeth.

'The strange thing is, is that in my dream Colin's wife Elizabeth is Jane's sister. My dreams are set in the 17th century and Colin's wife is talking in old English.'

Don thought for a while, then added, 'I remember reading a book once, it was called *Green Darkness*, and I think it was by Anya Seton. It was about past life regression. It's a story of undying love that combines mysticism, suspense, mystery, and romance into a web of good and evil that stretches from 16th-century England to the present day. Richard Marsdon marries a young American woman named Celia, and brings her to live at his English estate, and all seems to be going well. But now, Richard has become withdrawn, and Celia is constantly haunted by a vague dread. When she suffers a breakdown and wavers between life and death, a wise doctor realises that only by forcing Celia to relive her past can he enable her to escape her illness. Celia travels back 400 years in time to her past life as a beautiful but doomed servant. I think that Elizabeth has the same problem and I think you have a part to play.'

'All sounds a bit far-fetched to me, but you may be right. So, what do we do?'

'You need to do a bit of research on past life regression and then try to find a local practitioner.'

'Drink up, we'll go back to my place and check it out.'

They called for a taxi and after 30 minutes research on the computer they had found a past life regression practitioner in St Albans, (her name) Carolyn Proctor.

'I'll call her tomorrow,' says Nick as Don left to make the short walk home.

Nick phoned Carolyn on Friday and after a long discussion he made an appointment for Monday evening. He then had to contact Colin and persuade him. I'll wait till this evening and catch him at the Mermaid after work, he thought. Nick, never, if he could help it, teach on a Friday afternoon, it's just a waste of time. Therefore, he spent the afternoon preparing himself for the weekend. He changed into something more comfortable, light brown chinos and a t-shirt sporting the motto *If found return to the pub.* Colin usually arrives at the pub about 5:30 pm, and he had plenty of time, so he thought I'd watch a DVD and chill out.

He poured himself a glass of Laphroaig and started watching *Sliding Doors* staring Gwyneth Paltrow. He loves this film, and it really makes you think how a split second in your life can change you whole future.

The usual crowd was gathered and all sitting outside as the weather was still relatively warm. He ordered a pint of *Naked Ladies* from the Twickenham brewery. Not a bad pint at 4.4%, quite hoppy which gave it a real bitter taste. He found Colin sitting alone, joined him and explained what he had done.

'So, what do you think, are you up for it?' Nick asked.

'It's an interesting theory, but do you believe in past life regression?' he replied.

'I have an open mine, but it's worth a try.'

'Well, Elizabeth is getting worse; I'm at my wits end.'

'Okay I'll pick you both up on Monday.'

Ken, the landlord was collecting glasses, saw Nick and came over.

'Already for next week? he asked, all excited.

'Ready for what?' Nick had no idea what he was talking about.

'You're a card Nick, you know the quiz.'

'Just kidding Ken; what night is it?'

He was now starting to get annoyed. 'It's next Thursday.'

'Of course, it is, all in hand.'

'It'll better be, I'm relying on you'! He finished collecting the empties and stormed off.

'You hadn't actually forgotten it, had you?' asked Colin.

'It just slipped my mind; I'm more concerned with your problems.'

'That's nice; let's just hope they're solved before next Thursday.'

The three of them arrived at Carolyn's house on Monday evening. She lives in a prestigious part of St Albans. They were led though to her consulting room, a cross between a study and a lounge, it had been added to the main building. The room consisted of a large Victorian desk, a bookcase full of reference books on hypnosis, regression and the like. There was a two-seater settee and two matching chairs and a large recliner which

Nick assumed (rightly) was the famous 'couch'. The room was well decorated in pastel beige with a few expensive looking prints. They sat down and looked at Carolyn. Nick would say she was mid-forties, average height, somewhere between plain and almost attractive with shoulder length blonde hair. Carolyn spoke first, 'I have never come across a situation where more than one person was involved simultaneously. We could be onto something quite unique and very exciting. I am going to put each of you in turn under and see where this leads us. I think we should start with Elizabeth.'

Since Nick had picked them both up Elizabeth had not said a word, in fact you could say she was almost trance like. He thought it won't take much to put her under. Colin helped Elizabeth up and escorted her to the recliner. Once she seemed comfortable Carolyn sat down next to her and in a soft calming voice said -

'Close your eyes and follow the sound of my voice. It's time to relax. Take a deep breath in now, and as you breathe out, blow away any stress and tension. This time is for you, so give yourself permission to relax. Imagine now you are floating on a soft fluffy cloud. This cloud is filled full of loving energy. As you feel it all around you, fully supporting you, relax and let go. Your neck, head, and shoulders are feeling heavy, releasing all tension. The muscles in your face are relaxing as well as are your arms and hands. They grow heavier and heavier as the cloud helps you relax even more. The cosy cloud inspires you to relax all the tension from your upper body and lower body; give your body up to the cloud. Your legs and your feet are releasing every bit of tension now and becoming very heavy. You are becoming very calm relaxed and peaceful. So, as you drift even more deeply into a wonderful state of deep relaxation, your intention here is to view a past life and in a moment I'll count down from ten. Ten, nine, eight, seven, six, five, four, three, two, one. Where are you, Elizabeth?

No reply

'Where are you, Elizabeth?'

No reply.'

'Where are you Elizabeth,' she asked, for a third time, but now with added assurance. 'Answer me!'

In a moment she sighed, her blush lips moved, and we heard a faint whisper, 'At my sister's house on the Gorhambury estate.'

'What is your name?'

'Ellenor.'

'Are you happy?'

'No.'

'Will you tell us why?

1643

Ellenor's having dinner with her sister Jane they are having a Potage of Venison followed by apple pie. Her brother-in-law Sir Nicholas is there and their daughter Sarah.

'What troubles thee dear sister?' asks Jane.

'I'm not happy sweet sister, my husband Sir Thomas is such a brute of a man. I curse the day our father introduced him to me.'

'He seemed such a good catch, he has wealth, position and is very ambitious.'

'But he is not a kind and gentle husband; he treats me like a slave.'

'I cannot believe he would treat you that way.'

'Believe me, I can only take so much but he is the limit.'

'Please tell me sweet sister; give me an example of his wickedness.'

'He has terrible, vile habits in the bedroom. His hands are so rough I have sores on my delicate breasts and when he takes me it's so awful; I've seen dogs in the street with more finesse. And sometimes, I can hardly bring myself to say it; he makes me use a candle and pleasures himself whilst watching, as for his breath it is so bad it could fell a horse.'

'The scoundrel,' Sir Nicholas screamed, 'I shall run him though with my trusty sword.'

Ellenor started crying.

'Don't worry, dear sister we will protect you. You can stay here if you like'.

2004

Tears started to appear on Elizabeth's cheek.

'I think she's had enough for now, let's bring her back.' says Carolyn.

She looked at them, they nodded.

'In a moment I shall count you up and return you to normality, and bring back with you only remenbering the memories you wish to keep, here we go. One, two, three, four, five, returning healed and centred, seven, eight, nine, ten, and find yourself in your body once again. Take a deep breath in and out. You can open your eyes when ready.'

Elizabeth sat up and went back to her seat, she didn't say a thing. Carolyn looked at Colin, and said 'Colin are you ready?'

'As well as I will ever be,' he replied.

Colin made himself comfortable in the recliner. Elizabeth sat next him and repeated her speech. Colin went straight out; she's good Nick thought.

What is your name?'

'Conrad.'

What year is it?''

1643
Conrad is attending his pigs in the top field on the Gorhambury estate. He is very happy. He loves his job looking after his pigs, but it gets a bit lonely, since pigs don't have much conversation. Not that they aren't intelligent animals, but he would occasionally like some human companionship. But lately Lady Ellenor has been visiting him. She's the sister of his mistress and she's staying here for a while. He thinks she is sweet on him cos she's been up here talking to him every afternoon since she arrived. He doesn't think she is very happy as she tells him here husband is a bad man. He can't understand why anyone would treat a woman so badly. She is the most beautiful creature he has ever seen. He thinks, if she was mine, I would treat her like a princess and kill anyone if they harmed a hair on her head. But he can only dream and look forward to her visits.'

2004
Colin didn't say another word; he just laid there with a silly grin on his face.

61

'I don't think we'll get much more out of him,' said Nick. Best to bring him back.'

'I agree,' replied Carolyn, before she brought Colin back.

Colin awoke, 'What did I say?'

'I'll tell you later,' Nick replied.

Carolyn was grinning from ear to ear, 'this is fantastic, and we have got a definite connection between Elizabeth and Colin in 1643.' She was busy scribbling down notes. 'Now let's see where you fit in Nick.'

Nick reluctantly sat in the recliner. He was nervous, as he hates not being in control, but he thought it is for the best. It was a strange feeling, a bit like having an operation under a general anaesthetic.

'What is your name?'

'Sir Nicholas Capel.'

'What year is it?'

'1643.'

''What is your occupation?'

Gentleman farmer and Adventurer.'

'Where are you now?

1643

Sir Nicholas is in study of his house in Gorhambury. He is confused. He has a potential problem that he is unsure how to handle. Rumour has it that one of his farm hands, an excellent chap called Conrad is smitten with his sister-in-law Ellenor, and by the smile on her face lately it could be mutual. He knows she is married to that brute of a man Sir Thomas, and he's glad that she has found happiness, but he's worried that he might find out. The consequences could be very serious.

2004

Suddenly, he was back on the couch.

'I'm sorry,' says Carolyn, 'but the hour has gone so quickly, and I have to see another client now.'

Nick sheepishly went back to his chair. They all looked at Carolyn. She looked like the cat that had drunk all the cream and discovered she had two tails.

'This is brilliant,' she says.

So, what happens now? asked Colin.

'I would like to put Elizabeth under again. Do you think you could wait for an hour?

'Okay by me,' says Nick, looking at Colin.

He just shrugged his shoulders.

'Why don't you go into the lounge, I can put the television on if you like?

'That sounds great.'

When Carolyn returned an hour later, she was holding an old notebook. 'I've just remembered something I wrote down many years ago. Just give me a minute and I'll find it.'

The three just looked on as Carolyn quickly turned the pages of her notebook. 'Ah, hear it is. It was written by a Florentine historian called Francesco Guicciardini. "Whatsoever has been in the past or is now, will repeat itself in the future, but the names and surfaces of things will be so altered that he who is not a quick eye will not recognise them, or know how to guide himself accordingly..."

'Wow,' says Nick. 'Is this what we are dealing with?'

'It looks like it, but we must tread very carefully. We could do more harm than good.'

A few minutes later Elizabeth was back in the recliner.

1643

She is walking through the long grass back to the house. She had been with Colin. He took her into the barn; it was the first time they had laid together. He was so gentle; he removed each item of clothing so slowly and delicately. And when she was naked, he kissed and caressed every part of her body. He slowly ran his fingers up and down her curves just stopping short of her intimate parts. She was so ready for him. Then he entered her and even though he is hung like a donkey she felt no pain only pleasure. He did not hurry, just gentle rhythmic thrusts sending waves of pleasure through her arched body. Then something happened that has never happened before. She could feel something stirring deep down in her loins. As the rhythm of his thrusts increased so did the feeling; then it happened. She was overcome with pleasure. She wanted to shout the roof off. She wanted to squeeze this man so much. Then the calm came, he withdrew from her and rolled over. But he didn't fall asleep like her husband, he put his arm around her shoulder, pulled her close and she snuggled into his manly chest. They lay they for about ten minutes, it was heaven, and then she thought 'I could do that again'. So, she gently started to caress his manhood, it didn't take long to respond. She thought 'you are a big boy'. He started to move but she pushed him back, 'my turn' she said. She sat astride him and without any inhibitions she rode him to her heart's content. She could feel that feeling starting to stir, but this time she could control it. But when it came it was much more intense than the previous time. This time she screamed, she screamed so loud that every bird in every tree on the Gorhambury estate took flight. She thinks I love my pig farmer. I shall seek out my sister and ask for her counsel.

2004

They all looked at each other. 'You little devil, Colin.' Said Nick, smirking from ear to ear, 'didn't know you had it in you.'

If there was a competition for men blushing Colin would have won first place. Carolyn was also looking a little flushed; Elizabeth just laid there was a sweet smile on her face..

'So, what happens now?' Nick asked.

'I'll bring her round, I think she's had enough excitement for one evening, but come again tomorrow, we must find out what happens next.'

They said their goodbyes and Nick drove Colin and Elizabeth home.

After dropping off Colin and Elizabeth Nick decided he needed a drink. I'll just have the one as I was driving, he thought. He parked in the Mermaid car park and ventured inside, Rodney and Angus where there deep in conversation.

'Hello lads, can I join you?

'Of course, ye can laddie, let me buy yer a pint.'

'Thanks Angus; let's see what's on.'

He looked on the blackboard and checked out the guest ales and chose *Titanic Stout* for a change. Its finish is smoky, woody, hoppy, dry, fruity and quenching.

Ken came to serve,' what's it to be?'

'I think I could sink a *Titanic*,' Nick replied.

He winced.

'That'll definitely go down well.'

'Every bloody time we have *Titanic* on you come out with the same corny jokes.

'Sorry Ken, force of habit. Can I have some ice with it?'

Angus and Rodney were sniggering; although they had heard them a thousand times before, they love it when he winds Ken up.'

'Tell you a quick joke Ken,' says Nick.'

'Go on but make it quick.'

'Right; here goes. *There was a Jew and a Chinaman sitting in a bar. The Jew turned to the Chinaman and smacked him round the face, 'That's for Pearl Harbour', he said.*

'That was the Japanese not the Chinese', the Chinaman replied.

The Jew said 'Japanese, Chinese, all the same to me.'

A minute late the Chinaman turned to the Jew and smacked him round the face and said, 'That's for sinking the Titanic'.

The Jew said, 'that wasn't the Jews that was an iceberg'.

The Chinaman replied 'Goldberg, Pallenberg, iceberg, all the same to me.'

'God give me strength.'

'It's the way I tell them, Ken.'

Ken disappeared to serve another customer.

'You seem a bit high tonight, Nick,' says Rodney. 'What have you been up to?'

'You wouldn't believe it if I told you, but I shall.'

'Try me.'

So, Nick explained how he took Colin and Elizabeth to see Carolyn and how their lives were connected in the 17th century England. He didn't tell them the intimate details.

'That's extraordinary,' exclaimed Rodney. 'When are you going there again?'

'Tomorrow,' Nick replied, 'but enough about me. What's new with you. Are you ready for the quiz?'

'No problem,' said Angus, 'my mind is like a finely tuned encyclopaedia and Kate is still sober.'

'It's a week of miracles.'

'I'll tell ye laddie, I'm seeing in her in a different light now she's sobered up. She's quite intelligent and not back looking. I think I might ask her out.'

'You're nearly twenty years older than her.'

'What is age, it's just a number. Anyway, I think she has the hots for me, she likes a more mature man.'

Well, you go for it mate, but just be careful.'

'What do yer mean?

'Remember Mary, she threatened to cut your nuts off.'

Yer right, I'll leave it for a while.'

Colin, Elizabeth, and Nick arrived at Carolyn's the same time as yesterday and were ushered in to her consulting room. Elizabeth was first in the recliner. It didn't take long for Carolyn to put Elizabeth under

'Tell us what you are doing?'

1643

Elizabeth is her bedroom crying; her husband has just given her a good thrashing. She doesn't know what to do. She feels like ending it. She's back home after her long stay with her sister. Her husband has been away with the New Model Army, that's why she was staying with her sister. But now he's back and the moment she has been dreading has arrived. He wants her. His latest thing is for her to slowly take all her clothes, and parade naked up and down in front of him whilst he gets himself aroused. It was going okay until he stopped playing with himself, pulled her to the bed and felt her tummy. He had already mentioned she was looking a bit plump around the middle. It didn't take him long to realise she was with child. He knew it wasn't his, so he beat her until she had told him who the father is. After a few minutes she managed to drag herself to the window and saw him riding off in the direction of St Albans. She doesn't know what to do. She had surely betrayed by beloved Conrad, and he'll be dead before nightfall. She thinks, I'll take my own life and be with Conrad in heaven.

2004

They all looked at each other. Carolyn was the first to speak. 'Well, it is pretty obvious what the problem is; she thinks she's betrayed Conrad.'

'So, what happens now? Nick enquired.

'I'm not sure, just give me a minute.'

We waited; she was deep in thought.

'I've come to a conclusion.'

'Which is?' asked Nick.

'I think you are the key to solving this, I want you to go under again.'

Okay, if you think it will help.'

She brought Elizabeth back and they helped her off the recliner she didn't look well, Nick took her place and closed his eyes.

'Sir Nicholas, can you tell us what is happening?'

1643

Sir Nicholas is his study answering some correspondence when his manservant Ralph rushes in.

'Master, master, Sir Thomas is here. He's looking for Conrad the pig farmer, he doesn't look happy.'

'Which way did he head?'

'Towards the top field'

'Then there's no time to lose.'

He grabbed his sword, and they ran like the wind towards the top field. When they arrived, they could see Sir Thomas's horse outside the old barn where they keep bales of straw. Sir Thomas had corned Conrad in the barn and although armed with a pitchfork he was no match for a trained soldier like Sir Thomas.

'Leave him be,' Sir Nicholas shouted. as he entered the barn.

'Keep your nose out of this Royalist,' he sneered.

'He is in my employ therefore under my protection. If you want to kill him, you'll have to kill me first.'

'My pleasure,' he turned and faced Sir Nicholas.

Now Sir Nicholas is a good swordsman and the match for most men, but he knew Sir Thomas was better. They traded blows for a while as he tried to find a weakness. He was good and Sir Nicholas knew he was just toying with him.

'Is this the best you've got?' Sir Nicholas taunted him.

'Don't like to make it quick, I like to play with my opponent, give them a false sense of security.'

'Makes a change from playing with yourself.'

'You've asked for it now; prepare to die.'

This sudden surge came as a bit of a shock and the point of his blade cut Sir Nicholas's wrist causing him to drop his sword.

'Prepare to die Royalist pig.'

Sir Nicholas stumbled as he stepped back to avoid his deadly lunge. He was on his back when Sir Thomas lifted his sword to finish him off. A sickly grin came over his face as Sir Nicholas frantically reached out trying to find a weapon. But his luck was in as Conrad thrust his pitchfork into the back of Sir Thomas. As Sir Nicholas rolled over, he managed to grab his sword and thrust it deep into Sir Thomas's chest. He fell to his knees, took his last breath and was dead by the time he hit the ground.

'Well done sweet master, I thought you were done for,' gasped Ralph.

'It was never in doubt,' says Conrad.

They stood there for a while whilst Sir Nicholas got his breath back. Then Conrad gasped, 'What about Ellenor, do you think she will be alright?'

'How long will it take to ride to Hertford Ralph?'

'No more than an hour my sweet Lord.'

'Then saddle horses for Conrad and I; for we shall ride to Hertford, there is no time to spare.'

'What about Sir Thomas?'

'Dispose of the body Ralph; I believe the pigs need feeding.'

So, Sir Nicholas and Conrad rode to Hertford. When they reached Ellenor's home they were greeted by her housekeeper Ethel.

'Where is your mistress dear Ethel?'

'She was feeling unwell and has taken to her room.'

'Quickly woman, take us to her.'

They found Ellenor slumped on her bed; there were traces of a green plant around her mouth and leaves on her pillow, Sir Nicholas rushed over to her.

'Hemlock!'

'Oh no.' cried Conrad, 'Is she……. dead?'

'She is still breathing, but it is only a matter of time.'

'Is there anything we can do?'

'I'm afraid not.'

Conrad started sobbing.

Ethel stepped forward, 'I know a witch in Bengeo who has a cure for Hemlock poisoning.'

'Then I shall ride to Bengeo and seek out the witch.

'She is known as the wise woman.'

As he left the room Sir Nicholas turned to Conrad and said, 'Fear not my friend I shall find this witch return with the potion and save your beloved Ellenor. Oh, try and make her vomit, it might help.'

Bengeo is a little hamlet a few miles outside Hertford with just a few dwellings. Sir Nicholas dismounted next to an old woman smoking a clay pipe, sitting on a bench.

'Tell me old crone, is this Bengeo?'

'That it be, that it be'.

'Yes, it is, not that it be. You don't have to talk in that stupid voice to me. I'm not a tourist. I seek information about a wise woman.'

'Ah, the wise woman, the wise woman.'

'Yes, the Wise woman.'

'Two things, my lord, must thee know of the Wise woman. First, she is ... a woman, and second, she is ...'

'Wise?'

'You do know her then?'

'No, just a wild stab in the dark which is incidentally what you'll be getting if you don't start being a bit more helpful. Do you know where she lives?'

'Of course.'

'Where?'

'Here. Do you have an appointment?'

'No.'

'Well, you can go in anyway.'

'Thank you, old crone, here is a gold sovereign... which I'm not going to give to you.'

Sir Nicholas entered a cave, it was dark, very dark……

2004

'What happened next? Carolyn asked.

Silence.

'I'll have to bring him back.'

'What happened?' asked Nick.

Colin answered, 'Well basically, you've killed Sir Thomas, fed him to the pigs, Ellenor has poisoned herself and you have run off to find a witch.'

'Quiet evening then; so, what happens now.'

Carolyn looked thoughtful. 'We need to put Elizabeth under again, we need to find out if she dies or recovers.'

Nick stood up from the couch and Colin helped Elizabeth to get comfortable whilst Carolyn prepared herself.

Elizabeth went under straight away.

'Ellenor, where are you?'

1643

"Surrounded by friends
yet all alone
the one I loved
God has called home
the hugs of friends
helps ease the pain
and I know my loss
is my loved one's gain
but tears now flow
across my face
as I long for just
one more embrace
then comfort comes
and I see Christ's face
He hugs my loved one
and I feel God's grace".

'That's a death poem,' said Ethel.

'When I open my eyes, I shall be with Conrad in heaven, and we shall be together for ever. But I'm scared, deep down I know Jesus will bless our love because it is true and pure. But what if those bloody Catholics are right and I wake up in hell. No, my

faith is strong, and I shall open my eyes.......... Conrad my
darling you are here waiting for me. Are we in heaven or hell?'
    'We're in your bedroom. You haven't died; Sir Nicholas*
acquired a potion to make you better."
    'And what of my husband?"*
    'He won't be bothering you again, had a little accident....*
with a pitchfork.'

2004

Carolyn smiled and said, 'I think we've cracked it.'

Elizabeth woke immediately, smiling brightly, jumped off the couch and ran straight into the arms of Colin.

'What happens now?'

'I'll need to see Elizabeth one more, perhaps tomorrow. Just to make sure that everything is okay,' replied Carolyn.

Don and Nick arrived at the Mermaid about 8:30pm on Thursday and made their way to the bar. Nick looked around; the rest of our team was seated at a table, there were two spare seats.

'Two pints of *Black Angus* please Ken, everything alright?' Nick asked.

He looked worried, 'Kate's off her head already.'

'I thought she was on the wagon.'

'She was, but she is a bag of nerves. She's been drinking all day.'

'That's all we need; still we just have to make the most of it.'

We joined the team.

'All right lads.'

They looked a bit down.

'Come on,' says Nick, 'this is our night.'

'Course it is,' said Angus. 'We'll wipe the floor with them.'

'You alright Colin,' I asked. 'How's Elizabeth?'

'Yes, she's a lot better; got her last session tonight,' he replied.

'That's good, how are the other things?' asked Nick, nodding and winking.

'Not yet, but she is back in my bed.'

'That's a good sign; any day now then.'

'Let's hope so.'

There was a load screech from the microphone followed by 'testing, testing'. An overweight gentleman with a round face who introduced himself as Tom, the Quizmaster for the evening.

'Well good evening one and all and welcome to the first St Albans Pub Quiz. Tonight's teams are the White Lion, The Speckled Hen, The Crown, The Jolly Sailor, The Rats Castle and our hosts The Mermaid.'

There was a round of applause after each pub was announced.

'Now let me explain the rules; there are six rounds of questions, and one will be a picture round. Each round will consist of ten questions. Each team is allowed to play one joker, this will double your points for that round. The joker must be handed to me before your chosen round. Are there any questions?"

After the usual heckling, where's the toilet, what's the first answer and so on he continued.

'The categories for each round have been placed on your table but be very careful as some rounds are harder than others.'

We all looked at each other.

'What do you think?' asked Nick.

Not sure,' says Don, 'what about sport?'

'Always dodgy,' Nick replied. 'They usually ask questions about unusual sports.'

'Nick's right,' said Angus. 'Let's leave it for a while and see how we get on.'

The first round was on literature.

'Your specialist subject Kate,' said Rodney.

'Looking forward to it,' replied Kate, 'but must just go to the loo first.'

She somehow staggered around the table and wobbled her way to the toilet.

No one played the joker and thanks to Rodney, who answered most of the questions, they scored eight points. Kate reappeared.

'Right, I'm ready.'

No one spoke.

Round two was sport; the White Lion and the Jolly Sailor played their joker. Nick was right about the Sports round, the questions were very obscure, but Don and Colin did exceptionally well with some inspired guesses. They got seven correct. The White Lion got eight correct which gave them 16 points. They were now in the lead with 23 points. The Jolly Sailor didn't fare so well and only scored 12 points with their joker.

Round three – music. They were tempted to play the joker, but something stopped them. Nick couldn't explain what it was. They were happy with eight correct. Both the Crown and Speckled Hen played their jokers and scored 14 and 16 points respectively. At the interval the scores were as followed.

1.	White Lion	33 points
2.	Specked Hen	31 points
3.	Crown	30 points
4.	Jolly Sailor	26 points
5.	Mermaid	23 points
6.	Rat's Castle	19 points

They weren't too despondent during the break; drinks were ordered, and sandwiches appeared, and they still had their joker to play. So far Kate had failed to answer a single question, but she seemed to be enjoying herself more than the rest of them. Nick thought I couldn't have chosen a more competitive team if I had tried. What a great bunch of mates.

Round 4 was the picture round, and you had to be lucky with this round. The Rat's Castle played their joker, The Mermaid resisted. The picture sheet was handed out. 'Shit,' thought Nick, I think we have made a big mistake. There were ten pictures of characters from the *Harry Potter* films; he knew them all. Should have played the joker, still their first maximum points.

Round 5 – Entertainment.

'D you think we should play our Joker?' asked Rodney.

'What do the rest of you think?' asked Nick.

'You're pretty good at entertainment Nick,' said Don.

'Something is telling me to hold fast,' said Colin.

'I'm getting the same feeling,' agreed Angus. 'Since you have been involved in this regression lark, I'm getting some weird feelings.'

'Tell me about,' added Nick. 'Okay we'll hold it to the last round.'

Kate had now passed out. They worked well together and managed eight points. The Crown and White Lion scored maximum points.

'Check the score Rodney, how many do we need to win?' Nick asked.

'As it stands, we are last, ten points behind. All the other teams have played their jokers. If we get maximum points, we could still win.'

Kate was still fast asleep, but even worse, she was snoring. Tom, the quizmaster was, now getting into position.

'Are you ready for the last round? Still all to play for; the last round is Potluck. I see that the Mermaid have decided to play their Joker; so good luck to you all.'

'Question 1 - Which DJ played the first record on Radio One?'

'Standard question,' whispered Nick 'Tony Blackburn.'

Everybody agreed.

'Question 2 – In which two bond films did the villain Jaws appear?'

'Carry on like this and we have a chance – Moonraker and The Spy Who Loved Me, all agree,' says Nick.

The team all smiled and nodded. Kate's snoring was getting louder and someone from the opposition was throwing peanuts at her.

'Question 3 - Which Artist first took Unchained Melody to Number One in the charts?'

'I know this,' Nick exclaimed, 'Jimmy Young.'

'Are you sure laddie?" asked Angus.

'It's my favourite song, not that version of course. Trust me I'm a lecturer.'

Nick was really getting excited; his heart was pounding and his mouth drying out quicker than a baby's nappy in a dessert.

'Question 4 - What was the former name of Iceland?'

Silence, everyone was shaking their head.

'For crying out loud we're trying to think here, can't you stop that silly cow from snoring?' shouted a member from the White Lion team. Colin, who was sitting next to Kate, gave her a quick prod.

'Sorry about that,' said Kate. 'Must have dropped off for a second; what was the question?'

'What was the former name of Iceland?' said Rodney, who was sitting on her other side.

'Easy,' she replied, 'Bejam.' Then she went back to sleep.

'Good girl,' said Colin. as he planted a big kiss on the cheek of the lifeless body beside him.

'Question 5 - What colour shirts did Manchester United wear in the 1968 European Cup Final?'

'Easy,' said Don, 'It was blue; Nick bought me the exact replica shirt a few years ago for Christmas.'

Halfway there I thought, if only the next five are as easy. Nick looked to the heavens and whispered a short prayer.

'Question 6 - British Lop, Landrace, Middle White are all breeds of what type of farmyard animal?'

We all turned to Colin, he just smiled and nodded. Don wrote 'Pigs' on the answer sheet.

'Question 7 - What is a Sgian Dubh?'

'What the fuck is that?' asked Colin.

'It's a wee black dagger,' smirked Angus.

'Question 8 - What type of food is a Bombay Duck?'

They all laughed; oh, how we love our Indian food. Don wrote 'a small, dried fish.'

'My daughter calls them "Fanny Sticks",' says Nick.

The team laughed.

'Question 9 - Which author wrote the Agatha Raisin series of books?

Rodney was first to speak "Agatha, dear Agatha, oh how I love thee…. M.C.Beaton"

The last question I thought, if we get this right we have definitely won.

Last question: question 10 - What year saw the start of the English Civil War?'

We gave out an almighty roar; the Gods have surely been kind to us tonight. Don confirmed the answer - 1642 wrote it down and handed in our answer sheet. We gave Kate a good shove to wake her up as we waited patiently for the answers and the results. Ken came rushing over.

'How do you think you have done?' he asked all excited.

'Fingers crossed,' says Nick, 'but it should be in the bag.'

'Do you need any more drinks, on the house?'

I looked around they all nodded.

'Same again them and a large black coffee for Kate.

Ken brought over the drinks and waited with us whilst the answers and results were read. Tom got back to his position, tapped on the mike and said, 'Quiet please, here are the answers to round 10, Potluck.'

We knew that all our answers were correct, and we cheered loudly as each answer was read out.

'And now the final results,' announced Tom. 'In joint 5th place with 50 points – The Jolly Sailor and the Rats Castle"

They all gave a round of applause.

'In fourth place with 53 points – The Speckled Hen.'

More applause.

'In third place with a very respectable 54 points – The Crown.'

More applause.

'Now the moment you have all been waiting for, just one point separating the top two teams. The White Lion have 60 points, but the Mermaid has piped them with 61 points. Congratulations Mermaid.' The pub erupted; Ken was screaming at the top of his voice. All the other teams came over to congratulate them, as Tom tried to get order so he could present the trophy. It took him at least five minutes but eventually they settled down enough to hear him say, 'quiet please just for a moment. I would like to present this lovely trophy to the captain of the winning team. Could you please make your way up?"

They all looked at each other and nodded.

Up you go Kate,' says Nick. 'We voted you captain.'

A little shocked but beaming like a Cheshire cat she somehow managed to walk to Tom and collected our trophy. She raised it above her head and received the loudest cheer of the night.

Unbeknown to the group, amongst the mayhem Elizabeth had entered the pub. She bought herself a drink but stayed out of their sight. After the presentations were over, she approached our table.

'Looks like you've had a good night,' she says.

'We've had a great night, got a bit lucky at the end though,' says Colin.

'Well big boy, your luck isn't going to stop here. Grab your coat; I need a good seeing too.'

In all my years I've never seen Colin move so fast. But just before he left, he turned to me and said,' thanks mate.'

'No problem.'

Apologies to Richard Curtis and Ben Elton for pinching a couple of their lines.

The Devil's Disciple

'Come,' he said, 'come, we must see and act.
Devils or no devils, or all the devils at once,
it matters not; we fight him all the same.
Bram Stoker, Dracula

The Devil's Disciple

The *Princess Louise* is one of the must-visit historical pubs in London. Situated in High Holborn, it is remarkable both for its sumptuous late Victorian work and an amazing modern restoration. It's 5.30 pm. and Nick Allen is sitting in the back bar sipping a pint of *Samuel Smith's Old Brewery Bitter* at 4.0%. He's watching a group of office workers who are celebrating a colleague's birthday. They are the usual shiny two-piece suit brigade and librarian looking women. But one girl stands out, early thirties, dressed immaculately in a beige Reiss two-piece suit. She stands about five feet seven in heels, and her shoulder length blonde hair is expensively cut, and her eyes are deep China blue. She notices him and gives him a little smile. In his hand he has a group photo which contains many of the crowd in front of him. His target has a red ring around his face; he spots him immediately. He wouldn't have been difficult to spot even with just a basic description. Slimier than Cristiano Ronaldo, and a pair of hands that seemed to be attracted to every female bottom on view. Nick had to wait about 30 minutes before he made his move, and by that time, he had downed three pints of some tasteless lager; what a philistine. Nick followed him downstairs to the gent's toilet, which he must say are a piece of lavatorial magnificence only exceeded in the *Philharmonic* pub in Liverpool and proudly signed by their makers, J Tylor and Sons of London and Sydney. Nick waited until he was in mid-flow, then walked past and gave him a little nudge in the back causing him to pee on his shoes.

'Watch it mate,' he yelled.

'Why, what are you going to do?' Nick replied sarcastically.

'I'm going to knock your block off.'

'Well before you try, you better put that poor excuse for a dick away.'

He quickly zipped himself up then swung a fist at Nick which was easily avoided. Nick stepped in and hit him straight in the stomach. As he started to double up, Nick grabbed his head and slammed it into his rising knee. *Shit,* he thought, I've got blood on my new Levi's. Nick then grabbed his collar and dragged him into a cubicle. Stuck his head in the toilet bowl and gave it a flush. He then pulled his head out, bent down, looked him in the eyes and said 'Now listen sonny, I hear you've been annoying the girls in your office, and that's not very nice. So, it stops here and if I hear anything to the contrary, I'll be back and next time I won't be so nice.'

He mumbled some sort of reply. Nick noticed that his nose was still bleeding so he shoved his head down the toilet again and gave it another flush. Nick returned to the bar, picked up his glass and finished his beer. The blonde girl looked at him and raised her eyebrows; Nick looked back and gave a little nod. She smiled and mouthed the words 'thank you,'

Nick left the pub and took the short walk to Holborn tube station; two stops later he arrived at St Pancras International. From there he picked up the next train to St. Albans. Nick just got comfortable when he received a text message on his mobile. It just said 'thanks dad x.'

The slimy git had been sexually harassing, among others Nick's daughter at work. She should have reported him to the HR department, but as a family they do not trust anyone from Human Resources. They think they lie somewhere between Estate Agents and Paedophiles on the evolutionary scale. She had discussed it with her husband Arnold (Arnie to his friends) who could and would have sorted this mess out but unfortunately, he works for the same firm, but at another branch. There was a good chance that he would have been recognized; so, Nick was given the task. He had no problem with that; after all it's a dad's job to look after his daughter.

Nick arrived at the Mermaid public house at about 7:00 pm; it was an unusually warm evening for late October, and he could see that most of the punters were drinking in the beer garden. Blind Bill sat alone at the bar contemplating his beer whilst his guide dog Cadbury slept on the floor. He needed to walk quietly past them so he could order his beer and disappear to the garden. But once again he forgot that loose floorboard; it gave up a small creek. Cadbury opened one eye, recognized Nick and within a split second he had got to his feet and leapt at him, dragging his master off his stool, and landing him in a heap on the floor.

'Cadbury,' shouted Bill.

'Sorry Bill,' Nick said sheepishly.

'Oh, hello Nick,' he replied with a sigh.

Nick quickly moved to help him up.

'You got any of those dog chews on you,' he asked.

'You're not going to feed him after he's just pulled you off your stool?'

'No, I just want to know which end his head is so I can kick him in the nuts.

Nick produced a small bone that he'd bought on the market for £1.25; it'll keep Cadbury quiet for about 30 minutes. Money well spent! He had a quick chat with Bill, discussing the chances of Spurs finishing in the top six this season before venturing into the beer garden. But first, Nick ordered a pint of Belhaven 80 Shilling Scottish Ale. He'd grown quite fond of Scottish beers since Ken brewed his award-winning Black Angus. 80 Shilling is a classic, and is renowned for its luscious tart gooseberry fruit aroma and palate, balanced by toasted malts and spicy hops.

There seemed to be some sort of celebration going on and Rodney was the centre of attraction. He spotted me and shouted, 'Hi Nick, come and join us.'

'You look happy,' Nick replied. 'What's going on?'

'I've got a job.'

'Fantastic.' Rodney has been out of work for nearly a year.

'Tell me all about it.'

'Well, it's with HSBC, in their Human Resource department, pensions.'

Nick took a sharp intake of breath, 'Human Resources.'

'Oh, come on Nick, your just prejudiced.'

'Only joking, I'm really pleased for you, when do you start?'

'Next Monday, they need me right away.'

'Where will you be based?'

'Bricket Wood, where Ambassador College used to be.'

'I know it; there's a Sports Centre there, I've played football there a few times. Nice setting.'

At that point Kate, the pub alcoholic, staggered passed. She took out her mobile and made a call.

'Hello……. yeh I would like to order a pizza….to the Mermaid pub…….yeh, that's right……….12 inch Hawaiian……… 6 or 12 slices? errrm, 6, I couldn't eat 12 slices………….30 minutes, okay, thanks….. its Kate.'

Nick looked at Rodney and they both laughed out loud.

'Wos up wiv you two?' Kate asked, giving us a dirty look.

'Nothing,' said Rodney. 'Hope you enjoy your pizza'.

They went over and joined Angus and Tristan. Tristan is a chef at a local comprehensive school, mid-thirties six feet tall and very lean, some might say wiry.

'How's your half-term going Tristan?' Nick enquired.

'Not bad mate needed a few days off. I'm working tomorrow though, doing a stock check; how's yours?'

'Just relaxing, nothing much planned.'

'Nick, interrupted Angus. 'I believe you have a birthday coming up soon'.

'That's right, all the fives, 14th December. Same day as Michael Owen, Chris Waddle, George 6th and Nostradamus. Oh, I nearly forgot Jane Birkin and Vicki Michelle'.

'Did I really need to know that?'

'Just thought you might be interested.'

'Anyway, what I was thinking was that we should do something special. It'll give you something to occupy your mind.'

'Does my mind need occupying?'

'Let me think, you're a widower who still grieving, you hate your job, and you are too old to play football. So yes.'

'When you put it like that. What do you have in mind?'

'Nothing really.'

'Bollocks, just tell me.'

'A pub treasure hunt.'

'Go on,' Nick sighed.

'There will be teams say……three or four people. You set the clues and they must find the pub. Then they get other clues that lead them to the treasure. Something like that. And Tristan can do a barbeque and cook a cake with 55 candles, and we can all celebrate your birthday.' He was now getting really excited.

'55 candles, we'll need a fire extinguisher. Anything else?

'And then you and I will meet two fantastic women who will be overcome by our wit and charm. Then we'll whisk them off to a hotel and we won't see the sun rise for three days.'

'What ARE you drinking?'

'I'll have a pint of Stella, thanks.'

'Unbelievable.'

'Sounds like a good idea,' said Rodney.

'I'm up for it,' said Tristan.

I thought for a little while before saying, 'Okay, it could be good. We'll have it on the Saturday nearest my birthday'.

Angus was right, thought Nick. It will give me something to do, and I'm still feeling a bit shell-shocked after recent events. It's a year now since my wife Jane passed away and I'm having trouble moving on. Also, I'm on a final warning from work which means I must keep my nose clean for a year and stay away from all those involved in my hearing.

By Monday morning Nick was feeling really depressed. He phoned in sick and went back to bed, but he couldn't sleep. He's knows it's safer to stay at home when he's in this mood. He felt angry, bitter and knows that he would explode if he went to work. When eventually he rose, made some coffee, and started looking at old photo albums. His anger changed to sadness as he waded through his wedding album, then all the photos of his two girls growing up, the holiday photos and so on. By the time he'd finished his eyes were red and his face sopping wet from the tears he had been shedding.

He then spent the next two hours with a bottle of Jack Daniels; He couldn't remember where the rest of the day went. Tuesday, he felt much the same. He phoned work again and told them his back was still bad and he wouldn't be in until next Monday at the earliest. On Wednesday he phoned his friend Don Patrick to arrange their usual Thursday night out, but he was informed that he was unavailable as his wife has organized a theatre outing with some friends. Out of frustration he phoned his daughter Sarah, who lives near Bromley, to see if he could stay there for a few days. She said she would love him to stay, so he showered and was on the M25 within the hour.

Nick felt much better as he drove back to St. Albans Sunday evening. Sarah and Arnie really looked after him. Arnie plays rugby for a local club, and he went to watch him play on Saturday afternoon. Arnie is thirty-five, five foot nine tall and nearly as wide; perfect physique for a rugby player. Nick doesn't know that much about rugby, but Arnie put himself about a bit and his team won. Nick was impressed by some of the tackles he made although his opponents were less than pleased. Arnie is also a great Real Ale fan, and they enjoyed an excellent evening in his favourite London pub, the Harp in Covent Garden. It used to be called the Welsh Harp until an Irish couple took it over. It has six real ales including Timothy Taylor's Landlord, Black Sheep and Harvey's Best.

Monday came and Nick felt well enough to go back to work. In the evening, he started putting together the Pub crawl. First, he made some posters for the pub; as he needed to have some idea of numbers. Then he spent time on sorting out a theme and clues. If all went well it should be a day to remember. By Thursday, with most things sorted he decided to go for a drink at the Mermaid and put up the posters. Don was once not again unavailable again, due to some work function. The pub was relatively quiet for a Thursday evening and when he entered, only Angus from his crowd was there propping up the bar. He looked pleased to see Nick.

'Well hello stranger,' he said. 'Where the hell have ye been?'

'Not been too well,' Nick replied. 'But feeling better now. What's new with you?'

'Well laddie not a lot.'

'How's Rodney getting on with his new job?'

'That's an interesting question. Something's up with the wee lad, but I cannae put my finger on it.'

'Well, it must be stressful for him; he's been unemployed for ages.'

'Nae, he hasn't been in much since he started the job and when he does it's like he is somebody else.'

'Explain.'

'He seems more confident in himself, which is not a bad thing, but he has an air of arrogance about him. He's got some new mates, and he always talks about them. You know, John said this, and Edward said that. It just gets on me nerves.'

'I think it's good that he's made new friends.'

86

'But that's not all. He's joined a club.'

'Joined a club?'

'That's what I said, some sort of men's club; sounds a bit poofy to me.'

'I expect he's just trying to fit in. I bet in a few weeks' time he'll be back to his old self and in here every night moaning about work like the rest of us.'

'Aye laddie, let's hope you're right.'

'So, what else is new?' said Nick, changing the subject.

'Not a lot, but your favourite local band is playing here on Saturday night.'

I looked at the posters on the wall.

'MacLaren Wall, excellent; are you coming?'

'Wouldn't miss it for the world.'

'In that case, you and I mate, the MacLaren Wall groupies.'

MacLaren Wall are a duo comprising of Mac MacLaren and Melaine Wall, they perform melodic pop/rock covers. Nick always had a soft spot for Melaine. They have a good following, and the pub was heaving when he arrived on Saturday evening. Angus was already there and had secured a good position by the bar. Nick acknowledged a few friends and ordered a pint of Coniston Bluebird bitter. It was CAMRA's champion beer in 1998 and at 3.6% it's a nice pale bronze beer to start the evening with.

'I'm looking forward to this,' Nick said, taking a long sip of my beer.

'Aye laddie so am I,' Angus replied.

'I heard a good joke today; would you like to hear it?'

'Go on I could do with a good laugh.'

'Right here goes - *Two Scots, Archie and Jock, are sitting in the pub discussing Jock's forthcoming wedding.*

'Och, it's all going to be grand", says Jock. "I've everything organised already, the flowers, the church, the cards, the reception, the rings, the minister, even ma stag night".

Archie nods approvingly.

'Havens, I've even bought a kilt to be married in,' continued Jock.

'A kilt?' exclaims Archie. 'That's braw, you'll look pure deed smart in that!'

'And what's the tartan?' Archie then enquires.

'Och,' says Jock. 'I'd imagine she'll be in white."

'Not bad' said Angus, not sounding too impressed.

'It's the way I tell 'em,' Nick replied in his best Irish accent.

The duo was halfway through their first set when Angus nudged Nick and said, 'I think we might be alright tonight, those two lassies have been giving us the eye all evening.'

Nick looked to the end of the bar and sure enough there were two very attractive women. One was brunette the other blonde, both early forties with good figures.

'Are you sure they are looking at us?' Nick asked.

'Trust me laddie, if we play our cards right it could be their lucky night.'

Nick smiled to himself, 'So what's your plan then Romeo?

'It's a bit crowded at the moment' he whispered, 'so we'll wait until the break, and then make our move.'

'And what happens then, we just walk up to them and start talking. It's a long time since I chatted up any women. I'm a bit out of practice.'

'Leave it to me laddie, just watch and learn. With my Scottish charm and some great chat-up lines they'll be putty in our hands.'

'Right,' said Nick suppressing a laugh 'can I hear a few?'

'Okay, try this - *There must be something wrong with my eyes, I can't take them off you,*'

Nick said nothing.

'Or - *Do you believe in love at first sight, or should I walk by again?*'

'Anymore?'

'Hundreds, how about - *Tonight's sky must be empty, because all of the stars are sparkling in your eyes, - or - If you could put a price tag on beauty, you'd be worth more than Fort Knox.*'

Nick just stared. As luck would have it at that moment Rodney walked in.

'Rodney, perfect timing, what do you want?'

'Carling top please' he replied.

'New jacket?' Nick asked.

Rodney was sporting a very nice, expensive looking black leather jacket.

'Like it? Bought it today, had a nice little win on gee-gees. £10 double, 4/1 and 5/1. £300, not a bad day's work.'

'I thought you had given up gambling. Does Fiona know?'

Fiona is Rodney's long-term partner.

'It's not gambling it was an investment. Anyway, Fiona's away for the weekend, gone to a jazz festival with a friend.'

'So how is the new job going?' Nick asked inquisitively.

'Great, the work's interesting and I've made some new friends; couldn't be better.'

'And I hear you've joined a men's club.'

'It's not a men's club, there are a few women. It's just a few like-minded people who meet after work, have a few drinks, and help each other. We discuss financial matters and relationship problems. It's a sort of self-help group.'

'And they give you racing tips.'

'Occasionally, but mostly they give advice on investments plus stocks and shares. Anyway, enough about me what where you two taking about?'

'Well,' said Angus. 'We were just thinking about chatting up those two beauties over there.'

'No chance' said Rodney turning around and looking at them 'Out of your league.'

Melaine had just announced that this would be their last song before the break, the song *Every day is a winding road'*.

As the song finished Nick noticed that Rodney had disappeared.

'Where's Rodney,' he asked Angus.

Angus looked round 'The cheeky beggar, he's talking to those two lassies'.

Sure enough Rodney was engaged in deep conversation with the two girls. They stood there stunned, the girls were laughing, and giggling and hanging onto every word Rodney was saying. The next minute the girls had grabbed their coats and were following Rodney out of the door. Angus turned to me with a shocked look on his face.

'Didn't really fancy them, did you?' he asked, looking downhearted.

'No, of course not; mutton dressed as lamb. Would you like a single malt?'

'How very civil of you, that would be very nice.

'Ken, two single malts please, large ones'

Nick decided to try and cut back on his drinking and only go to the pub at weekends (which included Fridays); and Thursdays if Don was available, and he was this week. They decided to visit a few different pubs, which would also help Nick write clues for the pub crawl. They decided to explore Bar 62. Ten years ago, when it was known as the Pineapple. If you ventured in there wearing a suit or similar it was assumed that you were either CID or from the DHSS; but now, it's a trendy wine bar. It consists of one large bar with an eating area to the right. Each table is neatly laid and has a nice slender vase with an exotic flower. The menu looked good but a bit pricey. One starter – a seafood platter – cost £12.20. There was a lack of Real Ales so they both ordered a pint of London Pride.

The second pub they visited was the Boot. This pub has always been a favourite haunt of the 'in-crowd' and looks exactly the same as it did forty years ago when Nick first visited it. Its low ceiling and exposed beams and a great selection of Real Ales make it the ideal pub. As a bonus 60s music was being played by a DJ in the corner of the bar. The DJ, who looked a lot like Nigel from Eastenders (round face, chubby, curly perm) had the volume at the right level so conversation could take place. Nick ordered a pint of Triple Hop whilst Don settled for a pint of Adnams. Nick sat there totally relaxed and remembered the halcyon days of the 60s when St Albans rocked to the sound of the Zombies, Cortinas and the Bluetones and Donovan who paraded down the High Street with his guitar strapped to his back. That was it; we're staying here for the rest of the night, thought Nick.

On Friday, Nick was feeling really good. His depression had gone (for the moment) so after work he went home showered had something to eat and got ready for a night out. He had a feeling that something exciting was going to happen tonight, so he took extra time in his preparation. He ordered a taxi and arrived at the

Mermaid at about eight. It was a cold crisp evening, a dry, clear sky and a full moon.

Angus was in his usual position propping up the bar. Nick ordered a pint of Bateman XXXB at 4.8%. Angus looked at me and nodded towards Rodney who was sitting at a table with a face as long as a kite. Now Rodney hardly ever sits down when drinking so we knew something was wrong. We sat down either side of him.

'What's up Rodney,' Nick asked.

'Nothing,' he replied.

'Come on mate, you can tell us.'

But before he had chance to reply they were joined by two men. They were both about mid-forties, neat haircuts, dressed all in black. Looked like undertakers.

'Are you ready Edgar?' one of the men said aggressively.

'Aren't you going to introduce them Rodney?' Nick asked.

'Yeh, right,' said Rodney nervously. 'Nick, Angus, this is John Dee and Edward Kelley.'

'Pleased to meet you,' said Nick, standing and offering his hand.

There was no response, so he sat down.

Angus moved so Rodney could get out. As the two men escorted Rodney out, he turned back and said to Angus, 'I'll give you that Beatles film back tomorrow,' and then he looked at Nick and said, 'you're right the third Harry Potter film is the best.'

With that they were gone. There was a short pause before Angus said, 'What the hell was that all about?'

'No idea,' Nick replied.

'I've never lent him a Beatles film; I don't think I've ever seen a Beatles film.'

'And he has never seen a Harry Potter film, he can't stand Harry Potter.'

'And why did he call him Edgar?'

'I think he was trying to give us a message.'

'Not again, is this the start of another adventure.'

'I sure think so,' Nick said in his best American accent.

'Okay, but where do we start?'

'Right, name all the Beatles films'

'No idea.'

'Okay, leave it to me as usual,' said Nick. There was a *Hard Day's Night, Yellow Submarine* and *Help.*'

'We can assume he meant *Help.*'

'Obviously and the third Harry Potter film was *The Prisoner of Azkaban.*'

'What does that tell us?'

'Well, the Harry Potter films are about witches. So, I think he's been taken by witches, he's a prisoner and he wants us to rescue him.'

'It all seems a bit far-fetched to me.'

'Let us look at the facts. He starts a new job in Bricket Wood. Bricket Wood is famous for having a witch's coven. He joins this group and his luck changes.'

'Still not convinced,' he said shaking his head.

'And those women preferred him to us.'

'You're right, they were definitely bewitched. So, what do we do, where do we start and where are they taking him?'

'No idea.'

They sat for a few minutes thinking, and then Nick said, 'We need a computer, and we need to do some research.'

Angus thought, then said 'I think Ken has a laptop.'

'Okay, sort it, as quickly as possible.'

Within five minutes the laptop was in front of them, and they had internet access. Ken insisted that he worked the laptop as he didn't like other people using it.

'Right,' said Nick. 'First look up John Dee.'

Ken did as he was told.

'Here we are' said Ken enthusiastically 'John Dee was a sixteenth century mathematician, astronomer, astrologer, occultist, navigator, imperialist, and consultant to Queen Elizabeth I. He devoted much of his life to the study of alchemy, divination, and Hermetic philosophy.'

'Just as I thought they have taken the names of famous wizards. Now look up Bricket Wood witches.'

'Got it,' said Ken 'The Bricket Wood coven, or Hertfordshire coven was a coven of Gardnerian Witches founded in the 1940s by Gerald Gardner. It was notable for being the first coven in the Gardnerian line, though having its origins in the pre-Gardnerian New Forest coven. The coven formed after Gardner bought the

Five Acres Country Club, a Naturist club in the town of Bricket Wood, Hertfordshire, southern England, and met within the club's grounds. It played a significant part in the history of the neopagan religion of Wicca.'

'Do you know where Five Acres is?' Enquired Angus.

'Obviously I've heard of it, but I've never been there, but I have an idea where it is. Ken, do a google search on maps for Five acres, Bricket Wood,' replied Nick

Ken obliged.

'There it is, Five Acres Country Club, Five Acres Avenue.'

'Good, now hit the Satellite button.'

'Will do.'

'What can you see?'

'Lots of trees, a swimming pool and a few buildings, it's not all that clear'.

'Well, if we go there, I don't think they will be walking about outside. So, we'll look for a building with some lights on.'

'Then what will we do?' asked Angus.

'Not sure yet, just a minute I've just remembered something. My daughter Sarah and her husband Arnie are staying for the weekend with their friends, Martin, and Paige. They live in Bricket Wood, and their garden backs on to Five Acres. We could climb over their fence and make our approach from there. So, we need to book a taxi there a.s.a.p.'

They arrived at Paige and Martin's at about nine, and quickly explained the situation. They live in a large house in a quiet cul-del-sac in Bricket Wood. Sarah and Paige have been friends since they were children and are devoted to each. Arnie and Martin insisted on going with them, but Nick told Martin that he should wait by the fence to help them back over. Martin found a couple of flashlights and a small Maglight. Nick, Arnie and Angus climbed over the fence and made their way through the trees to where they hoped the buildings were. Their search was made easier by the full moon, and they soon stumbled on an old cottage, and could hear sounds of music coming from within. All the low-level windows were curtained off, but one high level window had a light shining through it.

'We need to see what's going on,' Nick whispered to Angus and Arnie.

'I'll climb on your shoulders and give you a full report,' said Angus.

'Thanks for that,' Nick replied.

'Don't be a big Jessie, come on bend down and help me up.'

Nick crouched down and Angus climbed on his shoulders. He stood up slowly allowing Angus a perfect view through the window.

'What can you see?' asked Arnie.

'They're all naked, except for something tied round their waist and they're wearing masks.'

Nick asked, 'what are they doing and how many are there? Can you see Rodney?'

'Just a minute; I can see eleven, three women and eight men. One is just sitting on a highchair, looks like the leader. He's wearing a big goat's head; the rest are just dancing around.'

'There should be thirteen; with Rodney that'll make twelve, can you see anyone else?'

'I can see the Rodney in the corner, he's with another girl'.

'Are they naked?'

'No, they're wearing white robes.'

'That's good; it means the ritual hasn't begun yet.'

'What ritual?' asked Arnie.

'I think they are selling their souls to the devil.'

'Bloody hell.'

'Exactly, what else can you see Angus? asked Nick.

'One of the women is from Essex,'

'How can you tell?'

'She's not a true blonde.'

'What?'

'Top and tails don't match.'

'ANGUS concentrate.'

'Sorry, not much else going on. Wow, you don't see that very often.'

'What's that?'

'A ginger bush.'

'I've never seen one of those,' said Arnie, innocently. 'Can I have a look?'

94

'For god's sake, you two. We're not here to ogle pubic hair, what else can you see?

'The third woman has a Brazilian.'

'For Christ's sake, get down.' Nick crouched down and Angus fell off and rolled in the leaves laughing.

'Come over here,' Nick wandered into the trees. 'Right, now listen; we need to create a distraction.'

'What have you got in mind.' asked Arnie.

'I have cunning plan,' said Nick. 'We'll start a series of small fires. We don't want to cause a lot of damage, so we'll use the dead leaves. It should make lots of smoke. Then we'll call the fire brigade, the witches will panic, run out and we'll grab Rodney.'

'Good plan,' said Arnie.

'Right, Angus you start gathering the leaves and dead twigs and make piles around the cottage. Arnie nip back to the house and bring back some old newspapers, matches and anything else that might be useful.'

Arnie disappeared and Nick helped Angus with the leaves.

'Have you never seen a ginger bush before?' asked Nick.

'No' he replied. 'Have you?'

'No.'

After about ten minutes they had four big piles around the front of the cottage. Arnie returned with a pile of newspapers which they rolled up and stuffed in the leaves. He also had some firelighters, which were left over from the barbeque season. But best of all Martin had found a box of fireworks which he had forgotten to use on Guy Fawkes Night.

'I need to see what's going on,' said Nick.

'On my shoulders,' said Arnie.

Nick climbed up and looked in. There was a pentagram painted on the floor and a black candle at each point. He could see Rodney and the other girl in the corner. They had disrobed and were being sponged down. He remembered reading once that it is important to bath before any ritual could take place. We still have time he thought. He jumped down and said, 'this is it lads, light the fires.'

Angus and Arnie took the firelighters, placed them under the leaves and lit them. Soon the smoke started to fill the sky Nick phoned the fire brigade.

'As soon as the fire brigade comes up the drive, we'll smash the windows and throw the fireworks in.'

They waited about five minutes, and then they heard the sirens. As soon as they saw the headlights Arnie threw a large stone through the first window and Angus tossed in a firework. They repeated this with the other windows whilst Nick waited by the door. As the firemen jumped out of the cabin, the door of the cottage burst open, and the naked witches started running out. The fireman just stood there; mouths open, unable to move looking totally bemused. As soon as Nick saw Rodney, he grabbed him and dragged him towards the trees. Two of the witches chased after him but Angus and Arnie came to their aid. Arnie rugby tackled one of them and then knocked him out with a single punch to the jaw. Angus adopted the Scottish method of fighting, head-butted the other one, then gave him a good kicking. Once they were hidden by the trees they stopped and looked round. The last witch out was the one wearing the goat's head. He slowly removed it and looked around. Nick recognized him as the one Rodney introduced as John Dee.

Martin had heard the commotion and was leaning over the fence shining a lantern. They quickly scrambled over the fence and got Rodney inside. They wrapped a blanket round him as he collapsed shamefacedly in an armchair. The other three sat on a large sofa panting. Martin then poured four large Scotches which they quickly drunk. Then six pairs of eyes stared at Rodney.

''Where's my jacket?' he asked.

Angus was first to reply, 'Buggar yer jacket, you great Irish tosser, what the fuck do you think you were doing?'

There was a short silence before he replied, 'I think it got a little out of hand.'

'A little out of hand,' Nick shouted. 'Don't you know how dangerous it is messing with the occult?'

'I thought it was just a bit of fun,' he replied sheepishly.

Angus was just about to throw another barrage of abuse when Sarah stepped in and said, 'Let's all calm down, Rodney's safe, you three have enjoyed yourselves playing heroes. We need to discuss what to do next.'

'First' said Paige 'Rodney needs some clothes.'

'We'll wait a while then I'll nip back to the cottage, hopefully the witches will have gone home,' said Nick.

'Good idea,' said Arnie, hoping for a little more action. 'I'll come with you just in case.'

'Thanks, and Angus can stay here and look after Rodney.'

'But' said Rodney physically shaking, 'he'll just shout at me.'

'Aye laddie, I have one or two more few things I need to get off my chest.'

They all laughed.

'So where did you leave your clothes Rodney?' asked Nick.

'In a small cupboard in the corner, near where they were washing us down.'

Paige gave Rodney a dressing gown and slippers to wear and Martin poured out some more drinks.

It was about eleven when Arnie and Nick climbed back over the fence. Martin waited with his lantern so they could find their way back and Angus, Sarah and Paige looked after Rodney who had now fallen asleep.

They reached the cottage in no time, it was empty, the doors were unlocked, but it had an eerie feel to it. They decided not to put on the lights, just in case, so they used the flashlights, and they soon found the cupboard and Rodney's clothes, including his precious new jacket. Before leaving Nick had a quick look around, there was nothing much to see. The black candles still flickered, and he could smell the remains of the burnt-out fireworks. But something caught his eye; it was a piece of parchment on the floor next to the leader's chair. He picked it up, examined it and put it into his pocket, signalled to Arnie and they made their way back to the fence.

Once inside they woke Rodney up, he looked at them with a glazed expression. They gave him his clothes and he went upstairs to change.

'Did everything go okay?' enquired Sarah.

No problem, seems the witches have flown away.'

'What was that you found, Nick?' asked Arnie.

'Oh yes, I nearly forgot,' he said, pulling out the piece of parchment. 'This is what tonight was about.' He showed them the parchment.

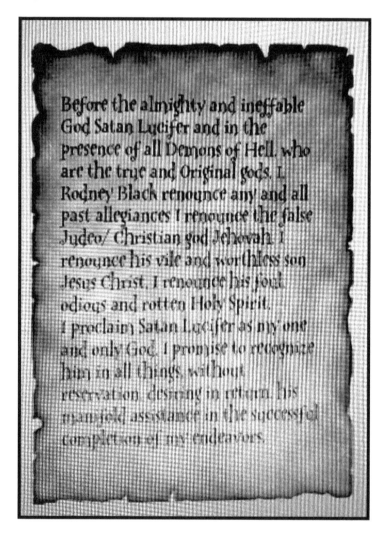

Before the almighty and ineffable God Satan Lucifer and in the presence of all Demons of Hell, who are the true and Original gods, I, Rodney Black renounce any and all past allegiances I renounce the false Judeo/Christian god Jehovah. I renounce his vile and worthless son Jesus Christ, I renounce his foul, odious and rotten Holy Spirit, I proclaim Satan Lucifer as my one and only God, I promise to recognize him in all things without reservation, desiring in return his manifold assistance in the successful completion of my endeavors.

'Wow,' said Sarah. 'That's really spooky.'
'I know,' Nick replied. 'You have to read it out loud, then sign it in blood.'
'That's evil, do you think he'll be alright.'

'I think we need to keep an eye on him for a while.'

'He can stay with me this week, Fiona's visiting her mother and won't be back until next Sunday.' said Angus.

Nick called a taxi, said their goodbyes, and thanked Paige and Martin for their hospitality and Sarah and Arnie for their help. The taxi dropped off Rodney and Angus at Angus's bungalow and then Nick at his empty house.

Rodney stayed with Angus during the week, he phoned HSBC to tell them that he wouldn't be at work due to a sudden illness. Each evening Nick stayed at home preparing for his 'Birthday Pub Crawl'. He decided that his original ideas were a little too complicated, so he settled for an easier version.

The rules where simple (he hopes)

Each team member must consume one alcoholic beverage at each of the listed St. Albans pubs.

- Blacksmiths Arms
- Boot
- Farmers Boy
- Farriers Arms
- Hare and Hounds
- Jolly Sailor
- Lower Red Lion
- Peacock
- Portland Arms
- Six Bells
- White Hart Tap
- White Lion

Each team must be present for a group photo outside each pub, as evidence of attending.

When purchasing your alcoholic drinks the landlord/bar person will issue you with a number.

The number represents a letter in the pub's name. i.e. Number 3 in Mermaid represents R.

Once you have collected all the letters rearrange them into the name of St Albans Pub that sadly no longer exists.

The winning team will be the first to present to Nick a team photo outside the shop that stands on the site of the mysterious pub.

The final beverage must be Champagne (or a cheap sparkling alternative) to be consumed during the final photo shoot.

It was arranged that the teams would meet at the Mermaid at 12 noon. Teams would register and be given instructions . The pub crawl would start at 12:30; allowing three pubs an hour plus finding the mysterious pub, they decided to light the barbeque at 5:00 pm.

Each team consisted of 3 members all must be in fancy dress. Nick would marshal events along with Don Patrick, Sarah, and Arnie. They decided to dress as superheroes. Nick chose an Austin Powers outfit which consisted of a Blue Velvet suit with a lacey cravat and cuffs and a pair of Chelsea Boots. Don's choice was a Superman jumpsuit with attached boot tops and 3D muscle chest. Sarah looked fantastic in her Wonder Woman outfit complete with cape, boot tops, tiara and gauntlets, finished off with a dark brown wig, Arnie thought he would look good as Buzz Light Year; his outfit came as a padded two-piece suit with detachable rocket wings, gloves, and headpiece.

At 12:00 noon six teams, fully dressed in costumes had arrived and were enjoying a complimentary drink courtesy of Ken the landlord.

Team 1 (Mermaid regulars)
- Angus Gold
- Rodney Black   All dressed in traditional Highland regalia.
- Colin Grande   (Angus insisted)

Team 2 (Mermaid regulars)
- Simon Prince (Mid-fifties, looks like Andrew Lloyd Webber)
- Diana (Slim, blonde, attractive 60-year-old)
- Blind Bill and Cadbury

Simon was dressed as The Phantom of the Opera whilst Diana came as Christine Daaé. Blind Bill chose a Sherlock Holmes costume with Cadbury sporting a pair of false ears to look like a Bloodhound.

Team 3 (Mermaid regulars)
- 'Ronnie' Barker (Mid-forties, real name Graham)
- Darren (Mid-twenties, well-built)
- Paul (Mid-fifties, Darren's dad)

All dressed as burglars, hooped jumpers, masks, and SWAG bags.

Team 4 (Art department, St Albans Regional College)
- Annie
- Polly   All dressed as fairies.
- Jenny

Team 5 (Friends from Cricket Club, all go by their nicknames)
- Jock – 1920s Footballer
- Rookie – 1920s Golfer
- T.P.O. (The Platinum One) – 1920s cricketer

Team 6 (Friends from Cricket Club, all go by their nicknames)
- Tiny Tim
- Jonty   All wearing Liverpool F.C. kit.
- Wilks

'What do you think?' asked Nick.
'Not bad laddie, I was expecting a few more teams but it's not a bad turn out,' replied Angus nervously.
'Where are you going to start?'
'I thought the Six Bells, it's the furthest away, then the Lower Red, Portland, Farriers etc.'
'Good plan.'
'Yer wee lassie looks good in her outfit.'
'Yes, takes after her mother. They both would look good in bin bags.'
'I see Kate hasn't made an appearance.'

'Did she say she was coming?' Nick replied, now getting worried.

'Aye, I'm afraid she did. But she's most probably still sleeping off last night's session.'

At 12:30 pm on the dot all the teams left the Mermaid in different directions gasping for their second drink. Nick paired up with his daughter Sarah to marshal the north side of town whilst Don and Arnie took the South side. They would keep in contact by mobile phone in case of any trouble. Once the pub was empty Sarah and Nick popped across the road to the Peacock. Team 3 – the burglars – were in there and they joined them. They were in deep conversation when Kate appeared dressed as a Hawaiian girl wearing a long grass shirt, a coconut shell bra and a four-piece garland flower set.

'Sorry I'm late,' she said gasping for breath. 'Can I join your team?'

'As much as we would love to have you,' said Darren sympathetically. 'The rules say only three to a team; so, I'm afraid the answer is NO.'

'Oh, you are such a tease Darren; come on, who's going to buy me a drink?'

Nick looked at Sarah, she nodded, and he said, 'Well we'll leave you to it, other pubs to marshal' and quickly made their exit.

They made their way to the Blacksmiths Arms and once at the bar looked around to see if any of their teams were there. They noticed that Team 4 – the Fairies – seemed to be enjoying themselves, attracting the attention of some fit looking youths. Or so they thought; actually, they were making some rather obscene remarks, which the fairies took offence to. The fairies then decided that enough was enough and threw their drinks over them. Sarah and Nick rushed over and managed to usher the fairies out before the unruly youths could cause any more trouble.

Don phoned and reported that Team 6 – Liverpool F.C - had reached the Hare and Hounds and Sky Sports were showing Arsenal v Liverpool. What started off as friendly banter with a group of Arsenal fans ended up as a free-for-all and the police were called in. The police also found that Tiny Tim's rucksack contained numerous beer glasses. In his statement he stated he couldn't help himself, it's a generic condition that affects people born in Liverpool.

Nick phoned Simon to see how Team 2 where doing and he reported that they had reached the Jolly Sailor where the barmaid thought it was a good idea to give Cadbury a bowl of water, but unfortunately some drinker kicked the bowl over, so he replaced the water with his strong lager. Cadbury was last seen making amorous advantages to a rather attractive French poodle.

Ronnie then phoned to report Team 3's progress; apparently eager to get rid of Kate, Darren suggested that they visit the White Hart Tap. But unfortunately, she tagged along. Once they arrived and ordered their drinks Kate insisted, they sat in the garden so that she could have a cigarette. She was just finishing her story of how Colonel Sanders, who used to be Elvis Presley's manager, became one of the world's richest men by putting an addictive chemical in his special recipe for Kentucky Fried Chicken to make us crave for more, when she accidentally set fire to her grass shirt with her cigarette. Without thinking, Darren, Paul, and 'Ronnie', threw their pints over her to extinguish the fire. She had to be treated for shock and minor burns to her legs at the local A & E.

By now Nick was getting a little worried and Sarah suggested that he should try to contact the other teams just to make sure that they were okay. He managed to get hold of Rookie who informed him that Team 5 was progressing nicely and had reached the Six Bells. Then Jock got word that Watford F.C. was victorious in their lunchtime kick-off and had decided to celebrate by hitting the top shelf. Despite their best efforts he and T.P.O. could not drag him away and at that moment Jock was on a table singing his own version of 'Watford the Brave'.

It was about 3:00pm when Nick received a call on his mobile, it was Angus.

'Nick,' he said. 'I'm struggling a bit here. Was there a team of Death Eaters?'

'No, why?'

'Because there are three sitting in the pub.'

'Which pub are you at?'

'Farriers Arms.'

'These Death Eaters, do you recognize them?'

'Of course not, they're wearing masks, stupid.'

'Calm down mate.'

'Sorry Nick, too much to drink.'

'Is Rodney okay?'

'Yeh, just gone to the bog; hang on the Death Eaters are following him.'

'The gents at the Farriers are outside,' Nick shouted down the phone. 'Angus, quickly follow them.'

Nick waited, thirty seconds later Angus called back.

'They've taken him.'

'Get after them' Nick shouted.

'I'm too drunk to run.'

'Then get Colin to go after them.'

Nick phoned Don and Arnie and asked them their location, as luck would have it, they were at the Boot. Nick told them to make their way to the Farriers Arms. He and Sarah were at the Lower Red Lion. Both pubs were in close proximity. Colin then phoned Nick to say he had spotted them going into the Maltings multi-storage car park which was between the two pubs. Nick then phoned Don and told him to go to the car park and they would meet them there. When Sarah and Nick arrived Arnie and Don were waiting at the exit. Nick phoned Colin and he informed us that the Death Eaters were on the second floor. They were driving a black BMW and were heading towards the exit. He also said the car would be easy to spot, the number plate was DEV 1L. They waited by the exit barrier out of sight. One of the Death Eaters, the driver had taken his mask off, and Nick recognized him as John Dee. As soon as he stopped the car and wound his window down to insert his ticket, they pounced. Arnie reached in and grabbed him by the ears and tried to pull him through the window. Don and Nick went for the back doors; Don pulled out Rodney on one side whilst Nick grabbed the other Death Eater out of the other. When the Death Eater, in the front passenger seat, tried to open his door Sarah kicked it shut trapping his hand. John had managed to open his door, which unbalanced Arnie and he fell back losing his grip on his ears. In a fit of rage, the other Death Eater had managed to open his door and push his way passed Sarah. Nick's opponent had scrambled to his feet and all three run off towards the market. Nick told Colin who now appeared, panting after running down the stairs, to take Rodney back to the Mermaid while the four of them pursued the Death Eaters.

Seen in the Herts Advertiser

DEATH EATERS NO MATCH FOR SUPERHEROES

Shoppers in St Albans Market came in for a surprise last Saturday when three male adults dressed as Death eaters (from the Harry Potter films) were pursued by four Superheroes. Local resident Sidney Hamilton, 66, described what happened "I was just buying my fruit and veg when someone pushed by me. I looked round and saw three death-eaters running through the market; they were being chased by Austin Powers, Superman. Buzz Light-Year and Wonder Woman. Buzz was in front and he rugby tackled a Death Eater and laid into him good and proper. The other two Death Eaters then turned round to help him, but Wonder Women knocked out one of them with some fancy high kicking and the third didn't stand a chance against Austin Powers and Superman. Then the police came and took the Death Eaters away."

Detective Sergeant Kevin Blakley stated that three adult males had been arrested and charged with attempted kidnap. He added that Nick Allen aka Austin Powers was known to the police and had assisted them in solving previous cases.

It was about 6:00pm when the last team returned to the *Mermaid*. Tristan had provided a splendid barbeque and the teams, despite being a little fragile, tucked in to a hearty meal. Others had joined them and listened intensely as each team told stories of their adventures. The eventual winners were Team Three, Darren's dad Paul easily re-arranged the letters to form The *Painters Arms* and remembered from his youth that it was situated at the top of the town.

Rodney decided not to go back to HSBC at Bricket Wood and stated he would look for another job after Christmas. As for Nick, he is now 55 years old now; perhaps he should look for another job. But as Rodney said, I'll wait till after Christmas.

Murder at the Mermaid

"It was the best of times; it was the worst of times".
"Was it f**k"

Murder at the Mermaid

April 2020

It was the third week of Boris Johnson's lockdown due to the Corona virus and Nick Allen, a retired college lecturer was stir crazy. There was only so much housework and gardening one can do in a day. He was missing all the things that he enjoyed, the socialising, his keep-fit classes, going to the theatre, the cinema and watching his beloved Spurs. But this evening would be different. The manager of his local pub, Jacob, had organised an illegal lock-in. The landlords John and Mark have turned a blind eye but applauded his initiative. It would be great to see his mates again. So, with a spring in his step, he drove his Nissen Note from his Victorian cottage in Frogmore to his favourite pub, The Mermaid in St. Albans. The streets were empty as he drove down the A5183 towards the Park Street roundabout.

'That must be a first' he thought as he drove straight across without stopping. Turning right at the King Harry he continued up Holywell Hill towards St. Peters Street. It was quite spooky driving through the main shopping centre with no one around. He half expected to see Simon Pegg and Nick Frost being chased by a horde of zombies. Turning right at the Blacksmiths Arms he drove slowly past the Mermaid turned right and parked his car besides Loreto College. After a short walk Nick was outside the pub. Nonchalantly, he glanced around, seeing no one he slipped into the car park and made his way to the back door. Two knocks followed by three more and the door was opened.

'You made it,' said Jacob the young manager in his twenties who had a degree in Marine Biology.

'Wild horses wouldn't have stopped me coming,' replied Nick still smiling.

'What are you drinking?

'You know what I like, surprise me'.

'How about Melford Mild? Its dark and from your favourite brewery – Nethergate.'

'Sounds good.'

Nick looked around. The only other customers were a retired train driver, affectionately known as Dave Train and someone of similar age to Dave who he vaguely recognised. He later found out his name was Clive.

'Hi Dave,' said Nick, 'still drinking that Citra shit.'

'Lot better than that rubbish you're sipping,' replied Dave.

'Whatever.'

'You know, you're the only Spurs fan that I actually like.'

'Well thank you Dave, from you I take that as a compliment. Still, now we know that there won't be a St. Totteringham day this year I'm happy. So are you going to introduce me to your mate.'

''S'pose. This is my neighbour Clive. He's not a big drinker, but he's getting under his wife's feet, and she begged me to take him out for a few hours.'

Clive nodded.

The secret knock on the door was followed by retired Taxi driver Paul. A pleasant fellow with a fine crop of grey hair and matching beard, Nick liked him a lot.

'Pint of Guinness Jacob,' requested Paul.

As soon as Jacob started to pour, the secret knock was heard again. In walked Nick's good friends Neil and Will. Will and Neil had met at teacher training college. Will was recently retired but Neil was still teaching. Both ordered pints of Citra.

'Any more coming?' asked Nick.

'Just your mate, Don,' replied Jacob.

Don Patrick was one of Nick's oldest friends.

'He's always late; he'll be late for his own funeral.'

As the last word left his mouth, he heard the now familiar knock on the door came and in walked Don Patrick, a retired financial director of a double-glazing firm.

Don ordered a pint of bitter plus a selection of crisps and nuts.

The Mermaid is a community pub, opened in the 1800s as a beer house. It has an 'L' shaped bar and is famous for serving an excellent range of real ales and cider. It has won many awards from CAMRA.

Jacob pushed two tables together and the men took their beers and made themselves comfortable, Don opened the nuts, crisps and spread them across the two tables. All but Clive helped themselves, eagerly stuffing the treats into their mouths.

'Not hungry Clive' asked Don.

'Not really, and I never eat nuts,' replied Clive.

Not wishing to pursue it Don asked, 'what have you been up to then, Neil. How have you overcome the boredom of living alone?'

'I've bought a bike and I go out once a day for my exercise. The problem is that I live on a hill and whichever way I go it's downhill, so that means when I've finished, I've got to cycle uphill to get home. Jacob, can you put some music on; you know what we like.'

'No problem,' replied Jacob. 'I've made a playlist especially for you lot. It's called Music for the Wrinkles'.

As Jacob disappeared to set up the music, Will asked 'what have you been up to Nick?'

'Well, when it's too cold to go in the garden I've been watching re-runs of 'Would I Lie to You', so funny. I love David Mitchell and Rob Brydon,' replied Nick.

'I think its rubbish,' said Dave Train.

'Were you born miserable, Dave,' asked Paul 'or did you take lessons?'

Before he could reply, Jacob who had finished setting up the music; 'You've Really Got Me' by the Kinks was now playing said, 'why don't we play that. You all think of a story – true or false, and we must guess whether it's true or not.'

'That's a great idea,' enthused Don 'and you can start Nick. You have more stories than Hans Christian Anderson.'

There was silence for a minute whilst Nick thought of a suitable story. While Jacob took orders for more beer. Nick noticed that Clive was only drinking halves. Once all the glasses were refreshed Nick started.

'Okay, when I was at school I had 'Cilla' ironed on my Jock Strap.'

When the laughter stopped, Paul asked 'explain how you got 'Cilla' ironed on your Jock Strap.'

'Well, back in 1964 there was a music magazine called Fab 208 and one week it had a free gift of iron-on transfers. So, I cut out 'Cilla' and ironed it on to my Jock Strap.'

Paul asked, 'did you iron it on or was it your mum?'

'Not sure.'

'Was it on the elastic or the pouch?'

A smattering of laughter.

'I think it was on the pouch.'

'Oh, I can imagine your mum saying, 'where would you like it, next to your willy or the left or right testicle?'

This was followed by a roar of laughter.

'Let's just say it was visible when I wore it.'

'Well,' said Jacob. 'Is it true or is it a lie?'

'Sounds like a load of old codswallop to me,' replied Dave Train.

Don laughed and said, 'let's put it this way, Nick used to be in the Cilla Black fan club, and he had a secret scrap book that he used to wank over.'

Nick blushed 'for fuck's sake, I never wanked over it. I had copies of Parade for that. But I was in her fan club.'

'So,' said Jacob. 'Is it true or a lie?'

'Well,' replied Will. 'After hearing all the evidence, we think it's true.'

Nick smiled and said, 'it's true.'

Finishing his pint Paul shouted, 'fill them up Jacob; it's time for another round'.

Nick said, 'think I need a pee' and made his way to the Gents toilet. At the same time Clive decided he needed to go.

'Enjoying yourself, Clive?' asked Nick.

'Not quite my thing, but yes it's okay.'

They both approached the Gents; Nick opened the door and walked through, Clive followed then said, 'I'm using the cubicle, I never use the urinals, I don't like them.'

Nick returned to the table; Clive arrived just after.

'Okay,' said Paul. 'Now we are all gathered, who's next? Don, how about you?'

Don scratched his head, took a sip of his beer and said, 'okay, I once asked Lloyds bank if I could have their cardboard cut-out of Jan Francis and they said yes.'

'Why would you want a cardboard cut-out of Jan Francis?' asked Dave Train.

'Because I fancied her at the time,' replied Don.

'So did I.' added Nick.

'Me to,' said Neil.

'Why did they have a cardboard cup-out of her in the first place?' asked Paul.

'If you remember she did a series of adverts with Nigel Havers in 1990, and they had a cardboard cut-out in my local branch. They knew me in there and I asked if I could have it and they said yes,' explained Don.

'So, you just took it home, bet the wife was pleased,' said Dave.

'So, what did you do with it?' asked Will.

'I put it in the spare room,' replied Don.

'Did you secretly have a wank over her,' laughed Nick.

'No comment.'

'So, what happened to it?' asked Paul.

'Can't really remember, just one day she was gone,' replied Don.

'Well,' said Jacob. 'What do we think, is it true or is it a lie?'

'If it's true, then he's a pervert,' said Dave.

'But she was gorgeous,' added Will.

'I'm not sure the bank would let him have it,' said Neil.

They all looked at Nick.

'I happen to know that it's true.'

Don nodded.

Dave Train stood and said, 'I think you're all a bit weird,' then made his way to the Gents.

Jacob made his way behind the bar thinking, this is going well.

When Dave returned and everyone had adequate liquid in their glasses, Paul said 'come on Dave you must have an interesting story to tell.'

'Nothing interesting to tell, I'll let you lot rabbit on,' replied Dave.

'God, you are a miserable old sod.'

'I'm happy the way I am just get on with your stories.'

'I've got one,' said Jacob.

'Excellent, enthused Paul. 'Let's hear it.'

Clearing his throat Jacob commenced, 'When I was at uni' we had a field trip to Cornwall, and I saw a Mermaid.'

There was a moments silence before Nick said, 'well he is a marine biologist, so he knows what he is looking for.'

'Bullshit,' said Dave. 'It's a lie, next one please.'

'Let him explain,' said Clive, who so far had not shown much interest in the stories.

Jacob commenced, 'as I said, we were on a field trip in Cornwall, staying at a hostel in Mawgan Porth. We heard that a rather nervous young man who had arranged to meet a mate one evening on the wide flat beach. The boys had intended to do some night fishing. They were looking for that great favourite of the Cornish dinner table, the Pilchard. On arriving at the beach, the boy was unable to see his friend. But he heard some rather strange noises coming from a large cave which at low tide is filled with large pools. Thinking that perhaps his friend was playing tricks he went to investigate. What he saw sent him running back up the beach. He was screaming blue murder and telling anyone that would listen that the devil had arrived in the southwest. He described what he saw as "part human" and had "long hair hanging about its body". So, the next day I went to investigate. I was standing on the cliffs at Bre Pen above the same beach. It was there that I saw something odd on the rocks below. There were three of them, sitting together on the rock, just offshore. Mermaids. They all had the upper body of a human, with pale skin. Their lower half was finished with a fin like a fish and was bluish in colour.'

'What did you do?' asked Clive.

'Well, I went back to the pub and told the locals. One said that he and his mates saw five the other day, it's a common occurrence.'

'Wow,' said Don. 'It sounds realistic to me; I think it's true.'

'I'm having second thoughts,' added Paul. 'I thought it was obviously a lie but I'm not so sure. Be great if it was true.'

'Come on then Jacob, tell us,' said Will.

Jacob replied, 'it's true.'

'Just one question, Jacob,' asked Nick. 'Were you pissed at the time?'

Jacob smiled, 'I might have been.'

They all burst out laughing.

'Okay,' said Jacob. 'Let's have one more, I've put some pies in the oven. They should be ready soon. So, who's next, it must be Neil.'

'When I was young, I tried to make some homemade beer and it was so lively that it poured out of the bucket and flooded my bedroom.'

'That's the sort of daft thing he would do', laughed Dave.

'I'm intrigued,' said Don. 'Please tell more.'

'When I was about 19 and had left school, I was living with my parents before I went to college. I was keen on beer and thought it was a good idea to brew my own with a simple kit bought from Boots the Chemist. After a few weeks it should have been more or less finished, but I was disappointed with the weak and thin taste. I wanted a stronger, more robust beer.

One night I went out to a local pub for a drink with a few friends. One of them heard my story and advised me to add sugar to strengthen the brew. He explained the science behind it and probably suggested an amount to put in. I walked home excitedly that night looking forward to making a big improvement to my beer. Checking the cupboard in our kitchen I saw that we had plenty of sugar, so I took a two-pound bag upstairs to my bedroom, which was where my "brewery" was. I had a large brewing bucket, about two foot six tall, sitting on the carpet with a good few gallons of disappointing weak brown liquid in it. At first, I poured the sugar in gently watching the reaction. Then I became braver when I saw there wasn't one. I needed to pee and brush my teeth, so I tipped the rest in and left the room.

Three minutes later I returned to witness something like the laboratory scenes from Carry on Screaming. My beer bin was overflowing onto the carpet; thick brown froth already covering an area of about three feet square, and there was no let up. I screamed, as if I had a part in the movie and my mum rushed into the room. Somehow, we got the bin into the bathroom and left it in the bath. I was in the doghouse for a few days and the carpet had to be renewed. Saddest part was that I never got to taste the beer.'

'Typical,' said Dave. 'Never could get anything right.'

'Excellent story though,' added Jacob; 'I'd say it was true, what do you lot reckon?'

It was agreed all round that the story was true, and this was confirmed by Neil.

Jacob shouted out 'food's ready', as the pies were dished up. Nick, Don and Neil went for the Moo (British Steak and Real Ale). Dave, Will and Paul chose the Moo and Blue (British Steak and Stilton), whilst Clive enjoyed the Kevin Vegan (Mushroom, tomato, Red Wine, with Baby Onions and Thyme). It was clear that everyone was having a good time, even Dave Train cracked a joke or two. It didn't take long to clear the empty plates and the boys waited in anticipation to hear the next story.

'Wait just a second,' said Dave, 'I need a quick slash.'

'He always does that, just when you want to do something he has to have a slash,' gasped Neil.

'I might as well go as well,' added Will, 'I haven't been yet, which is some sort of miracle.'

When Will returned, Neil said 'where's Dave?'

'I didn't see him, must be having a dump,' replied Will.

It wasn't too long for Dave to reappear, 'that's better, who's next.'

A short pause before Will said, 'okay, it must be my turn. Many years ago, I took a beautiful girl to Bosham. I parked the car on the beach and when I returned the tide had come in and my car was nowhere to be seen.'

'This sounds fun, tell us the whole story,' enthused Don.

Before Will could start, Clive stood up and said, 'sorry, carry on, I'll catch up,' and he disappeared to the Gents.

'Her name was Angie, and she was gorgeous, I drove down to Bosham, near Chichester in my newly acquired Hillman Hunter. I picked her up from her parent's house, drove to the coast and parked on the beach just off Shore Lane. It's a truly beautiful and picturesque spot and has an iconic church where, it is said, that King Canute's daughter is buried. We had a lovely romantic stroll and time seemed to stand still. We went for a late lunch in the Bosham Inn with beautiful views over the harbour. Even though the inn was festooned in old photos of stranded and sunken cars it hadn't occurred to me that I was in any kind of trouble. Nor indeed did I make any connection until we had left the pub and began to walk back. I looked around at the changed scene with a growing sense of panic. There was sea everywhere!!

No sign of the car, where I had parked nothing but gentle waves. How could I have been so stupid? Just to rub it in I now saw clearly the many signs warning motorists of the dangers of parking near Shore Lane clearly stating the road floods at high tide.'

Will paused for a moment before continuing, 'I will always be grateful to the kind folk of Bosham who must have pushed my car off the beach and onto the relative safety of Shore Lane. We were so lucky that the tide was up around the wheels but had not risen above the bottom of the doors. We had to wait a few hours until I could access the car and drive us back, but all was well, and it started first time.'

Everyone was laughing and making funny and rude comments to Will when Nick said, 'where's Clive, he's been a long time.'

'I'll have a look, I need the loo anyway,' said Jacob.

Everyone waited in anticipation for Jacob to return; suddenly he rushed out of the Gents and shouted 'I think he's collapsed in the cubicle. I shouted but he didn't answer.'

The lads all rose quickly and rushed to the toilet.

'Clive, Clive are you alright can you hear me,' someone shouted.

'We'll need to break the door down,' said Dave, 'Stand back I've always wanted to do this.'

There wasn't a lot of room, so the boys stood back in the bar. Dave lent back on the wall and kicked at the door; the lock gave way on the second kick. The door only opened a small way as Clive was slumped on the floor.

'Shit,' said Dave, 'he's on the floor and blocking the door. I'll try and squeeze in.'

'I'll do it,' said Jacob, 'I'm the smallest here.'

'No, leave it to me,' insisted Dave, 'I brought him here, I'll get him out.'

'Somehow, after a lot of struggling Dave managed to squeeze into the cubicle. Once in the door shut and the lads listened as Dave tried successfully to lift Clive off the floor and drag him back out into the bar. Clive was totally unconscious and had his trousers and pants hanging round his ankles.

'Is he breathing?' asked Nick.

'For fucks sake pull his trousers up, I don't want to see his shrivelled dick,' added Neil.

Quickly Nick helped to make Clive look decent.

'He's not breathing,' said Nick, 'lie him down and I'll start CPR. Someone can give him the kiss of life while I start pumping.'

Everyone stood back, Nick looked up when he heard someone 'I'm not kissing him.'

'For God's sake I'll do it, just phone for an ambulance.'

Nick started CPR and remembering his training started singing.

'Nellie the Elephant packed her trunk.

And said goodbye to the circus.

Off she went with a trumpery-trump

Trump, Trump, Trump.'

By the time the ambulance arrived Nick was in a sweat, and it was clear that his efforts had been in vain. Clive was dead.

The paramedics tried to resuscitate Clive using their defibrillator, but it was too late. They reckoned he must have had a heart attack whilst sitting on the pan. The mood was solemn once the medics had gone; most thinking it was time to go home. Jacob, sensing the mood said, 'It's been a shock, sit down and I'll get you something stronger, whisky anyone?'

'Jamesons for me,' said Don.

'Bells for me and Will.' added Neil.

'Laphroaig,' said Nick.

'Anything for me,' said Paul, 'I'm not much of a whisky drinker.'

'Or me,' added Dave.

While Jacob was pouring the drinks Nick decided to pay a visit. As he entered curiosity took hold of him and he entered the cubicle. The door was still intact although the lock was broken. What made him go in there, and what was he looking for? He made a thorough examination before leaving and then returned to his friends.

The mood was subdued but the conversation still flowed.

'I can't believe he had a heart attack in there, he looked so healthy,' said Neil. 'What do you think Nick? You're not normally this quiet, something on your mind.'

'Well, if you want to know what I think. I think he was murdered and one of us killed him.'

'Oh no, not again' sighed Don, putting his head in his hands.

'What do you mean?' asked Will.

Don gave out another great sigh, 'ever since we were kids, he's had this thing. He thinks he's a consulting detective.'

Nick looked offended and replied, 'I was a consulting detective, remember how many cases we solved. At one time we were quite famous.'

'Okay, we solved a few cases, but we were more infamous than famous. But unfortunately, Nick's instincts, however unbelievable, were usually right. So, I think we should hear him out.'

'Thank you,' said Nick perking up a bit. 'We all agree that Clive didn't look the type to have a heart attack whilst having a dump.'

'I don't think he had a dump, there wasn't any evidence of that when I managed to get in there,' said Dave.

'Not sure his bowel movements have any relevance to this case,' said Paul.

'Anyway,' added Neil, 'why would anyone of us kill him, no one knew him except Dave.'

Dave looked shocked, 'don't look at me. I didn't make him have a heart attack. It wasn't my idea that he came anyway.'

'Well Nick, are you going to reveal the killer and explain how he did it. I can't wait for this. Am I, your best friend, and also a suspect?' asked Don.

Nick gave a little cough to clear his throat; he was going to enjoy this. Memories started flooding back to his teenage years – his involvement with MI5, the mad geography teacher, Charlie Davies and Father John; even later when he found Lord Lucan's killer.

'In your own time,' said Neil, 'we're all in suspenders here.'

'Sorry,' said Nick, 'let us begin. Even at my age I haven't lost my powers of observation. My mind is always active, looking around, looking for things that just don't seem right. What intrigued me was how uncomfortable some of you looked when you saw Clive sitting at the bar. Neil, if looks could kill, he would have been dead hours ago. Will, you gave a shudder when you clocked him, and Paul couldn't bear to look at him. Even Don seemed to recognise him. You all looked like you wanted to do him harm. So, I ask you – Neil, how do you know Clive?'

'I think you already know, Nick. I told you a few years back.'

'Yes, it took me a while to put two and two together. You should tell the others, they'll understand.'

'Clive was the parent of a student I used to teach. She was fifteen and an absolute beauty. Could easily pass for eighteen and she had a massive crush on me. Well, she was only human. You'll never understand the willpower I had to resist her. It was on a plate, there for the taking. It would have been so easy. Did I fancy her, absolutely, anyone would; but I was professional, kept my distance. At first it was just little remarks that could be taken two ways. Then little notes tucked in with her homework. The sort of things you would find in a packet of Love Hearts. All Yours, Dear One, You're Fab and the like. But they gradually got worse; the last one said, "When Are You Going to Fuck Me". She tried to get me to give her a lift home, making such excuses as she'd missed the bus, or she had lost her purse. Once she had a genuine excuse, she was playing for the school hockey team after school, and she missed her bus. I knew she had a doctor's appointment which she would have missed if she had waited for the next bus. So, I gave her a lift home. She told me not to park outside her house, she didn't want her dad to see her get out of a stranger's car, so I parked round the corner. As soon as I parked the car and, put the hand brake on, she leapt on me and started kissing me. I was taken aback for a second, but I succumbed. It was wonderful, lasted about two minutes, then she stopped, said 'thanks for the lift,' and got out of the car. I just sat there, flabbergasted, with an enormous hard on. After that I started to bike in. Took me about 45 minutes each way, but it was safer. It was a couple of weeks later that I was called in to see the headmaster. He told me that Kylie's father; sorry, that was the girl's name, had been to see him. He said that he had taken Kylie out of school because she was pregnant and that I was the father. Also, he'd been to the police accusing me of having sex with a minor and the rest. I was staggered and protested my innocence. I was suspended and told not to contact anyone from the school (except my union rep), especially Kylie or any other student. I was suspended for four weeks before the truth came out. It was only because Kylie's best friend went to see the headmaster. It appears that Kylie never told her dad that I was the father, he just assumed it was. She explained that Kylie's dad had it in for me, as apparently, I had badly injured him in a Staff v Parents football match, a few years back. But what really annoyed me was that the real father was some spotty fifth former who was really ugly. There you are that's my story, a reason to kill him – yes. But I didn't.'

Nick patted him on the shoulder and said, 'that was very brave of you, and I didn't think you are the killer.'

Neil downed his Bells in one go and said, 'another one please Jacob and make it a large one.'

Nick looked around and said, 'Will, how do you know Clive?'

Will took a deep breath, looked at the faces of the other drinkers, not the happy smiling faces of an hour ago. 'My story might not be as dramatic as Neil's but the impact on my family was just as devastating. When I saw him sitting there, I really wanted to smash his face in. And yes, I'm glad he's dead and maybe I wish I had done it, but I didn't. Clive was my financial advisor and twenty years ago an old aunt of mine who I was particularly fond of passed away. In her will she left me the princely sum of £10,000. Clive advised me to invest it all in Northern Rock. 'This bank is going places, you'll make a fortune,' he said. 'Investing in banks is the safest investment ever. Had you ever known a bank to collapse, trust me it's a no brainer.' Shares were trading at about 200p, so I purchased 5000. At first, they climbed steadily then they seemed to rocket. In 2007 they had risen to about 1200p. My investment had grown six-fold. At this stage I wanted to cash it in, but Clive persuaded me not to, saying that they could only increase more. I thought with £60,000 I could top up my pension, put some in a trust fund for the kids and other things. But you know the rest, the bank collapsed, and I lost the lot. I fucking hated that bloke.'

'Well,' said Nick, 'that was interesting, I can understand why you would want to kill him, but you are not the killer.' Looking around, before taking a sip of his Laphroaig, he then turned to Paul. 'So, Paul how do you know Clive?'

'Clive is a little shit,' said Paul. 'Many years ago, when the kids were small, and like most couples money was tight. So, I used to work extra shifts at night to bring in a few extra quid. One night I got a fare to pick up some bloke, which happened to be Clive, from Ronnie Scott's in London. It was about midnight when Clive staggered out of the club. He was pissed as a newt. Luckily, he was fast asleep by the time I got to Old Compton St. The drive back to St. Albans was uneventful. I parked outside his house, had to get out of the cab to open his door and to give him a shove to wake him up. He looked at me then turned round and threw up all over the back seat. Then he collapsed, half in and half out of the cab. I left him there while I knocked on his front door to get his wife. She eventually opened the door, not looking her best I remember. She was fuming to see the state he was in. Together we managed to drag him indoors. She then ushered me out, I asked for the fare, but she just that it was not her problem and slammed the door. I never got the money and then I lost a day's pay trying to clean up the cab and get rid of the smell. So yeah, I could have killed him, but I didn't.'

The pub was silent as the punters sipped at their drinks. Jacob asked if anyone would like a refill, no one answered,

Nick broke the silence, 'Don, how do you know Clive?'

'A few years back I was driving down Beech Road towards the Ancient Briton. I pulled up behind Clive's' car at the lights and when they changed, we both drove off. He had just got to Batchwood Drive when he suddenly for no obvious reason braked. This came as a complete surprised and although I did an emergency stop, I still managed to give him a small prang. I got out to inspect the damage which I expected to be minimal. To my surprise it was a lot worse than I expected. We exchanged details and I asked him why he had stopped so suddenly. He said that a cat ran out in front of him, and he didn't want to hit it. Utter bullshit, I saw no cat. Not only did I lose my no-claims bonus he also claimed for whiplash, and I had to pay for his medical expenses. I also found out later that the damage to his car was done previously when his wife reversed into a wall whilst trying to park. I hate the bloke and I'll buy a beer for whoever did kill him.'

'So,' said Nick, we are down to just two suspects, Jacob and Dave Train.' I think we can rule Jacob out, so that just leaves you Dave, I think you killed Clive.'

'What, me! I don't think so, how could I have done it and what reason did I have?' said the flustered Dave.

'I think he was screwing your wife and somehow you found out.'

Dave reddened, 'what makes you think that?'

'Let's be honest Dave, you're retired, and you spend nearly every day at one pub or another. You totally ignore your wife and I've walked past your house many times and I've seen Clive go into your house on a few occasions. Haven't you noticed the flowers that kept appearing? Am I right?'

'Okay, I might be a bit selfish, but I'm not dim. I had started to notice a few things. How she looked flushed on the odd occasion I came home early. Then I saw a text on her phone that confirmed it. Yes, I hated the bloke, but I didn't kill him.'

''Oh yes you did.'

'Prove it.'

'Before I do, I must say how brilliant your plan was, If I wasn't here, you could have easily gotten away with it.'

'I'm intrigued,' gasped Neil, 'tell us how he it did it.'

'Okay, but I must say I'm well impressed. To start with you know Clive's strange toilet habits; he never uses the urinal and always pisses in the cubical. Even more strange he never sits on the seat, always on the pan. He is also allergic to peanuts. It was only when we dragged him out of the cubicle, and he was naked from the waist down that I noticed a series of red blotches on his arse. After he had been taken away, something compelled me to have a look in the cubicle. What I found was a small spec of Blu Tack on the pan and after further searching I found a drawing pin.'

Nick took it out of pocket and placed it on the table.

''While you were in the cubicle and before you dragged Clive out; you had to clear all the evidence, but you missed this one. If you look closely, you can see that it has some peanut butter on it. Your plan was to stick a series of drawing pins, with Blu Tack and loaded with peanut butter on the toilet rim. So, when Clive went for a piss, he would automatically lift the toilet lid and sit down. The drawing pins would puncture Clive's bottom and inject him with peanut butter. This would cause an anaphylactic shock and give him a heart attack, which is exactly what happened – the perfect murder.'

Dave Train went as white as a sheet. 'I didn't mean to kill him.'

'Fucking hell, Dave, I didn't know you had it in you,' gasped Neil.

'What you gonna do now, call the police?' asked Dave.

'We all know it was you, but we can't actually prove it and unless the police suspect foul play, there's not much we can do.'

'I appreciate that; if there's anything I can do, just ask.'

'Well, there is one thing that you've never done before,' said Neil.

'What's that?'

'Buy a round of drinks.'

Don't Fear the Reaper

All our times have come.
Here but now, they've gone.
Seasons don't fear the reaper.
Nor do the wind the sun or the rain.
We can be like they are.

Don't Fear the Reaper

2010

Philip James knew he was dying, and he knew that today would be his last day on earth. He kept looking at the door of the hospital ward expecting the Grim Reaper to walk in at any time. He wasn't frightened, he'd had a good life, and it would be a welcome relief. He had lung cancer and a touch of dementia. Sometimes he couldn't even remember who he was. But today, his last day on earth, his mind was clear, and the memories came flooding back. He was born in 1929 in Tottenham, North London and lived in Crowland Road with his parents and two sisters. Leaving school at 15 he took an apprenticeship with a local Engineering firm; and in 1950 he was called up for national service and saw action in the Korean War. When his time was up, he returned home and applied to join the Metropolitan Police. Three years later he married his childhood sweetheart, Eileen Green and their first daughter Denise was born in 1957. His second daughter Marion, two years later. Life was tough in the Met, long hours, hard and vicious criminals. He could see this was affecting his marriage and recalled how many of his colleagues' marriages had broken down. To avoid this, he applied for a position in the CID at St. Albans in which he was successful. So successful was he that by 1963 he had reached the level of Detective Inspector. He remembered his years at St Albans with much fondness, but with retirement looming he took the position of Detective Chief Inspector and moved to Norfolk.

Before he retired in 1988, his daughter Denise gave birth to his only grandchild, a girl, who they named Esther. She was the apple of his eye, and he spent as much of his time as he could with her. As she grew older, they become inseparable. She loved to hear the stories of his time in the police, and she always said that she would become a policewoman when she was older. Often, they would play a game of *Cluedo,* and he was surprised how often she would win. Sometimes after she had read an Agatha Christie or a Sherlock Holmes story, they would discuss the case and come up with ways the hero could have solved the case earlier. He always remarked how extremely pretty she was. Not that her parents weren't good looking, it was just that she was stunning. Her hair was blonde, both parents had brown hair and her eyes were a sparkling blue, again both parents had brown eyes. Is that possible? Every time he looked into those eyes it reminded him of a young boy he knew back in the sixties. He often wondered what happened to him. It was then he remembered and started to panic. 'I must see her before I go. It must be today,' he muttered to himself.

A nurse walked past and noticed that he was distressed.

'Are you okay Mr James?' she asked.

He beckoned her over and whispered in her ear.

'Right away, Mr James, leave it to me.'

*

Denise James, now Denise Robinson is preparing the evening meal for herself and her daughter Esther. Even though Esther is 25 years old, and engaged to be married she still lives at home. This is a blessing, since she lost her husband two years ago it has been hard, and Esther has been her rock. She doesn't know how she would cope on her own. She dreads the day Esther and Steve (her fiancé) get married and buy their own place. As she prepares the salad her phone rings. She quickly answers it. It's the hospital.

'Hello, Denise Robinson speaking.'

'Ah, Mrs Robinson, this is Nurse Williams from the hospital. It's about your father.'

'Is he okay, has something happened?'

'It's not good news, I afraid. Your father has taken a turn for the worse, the doctor doesn't think he will last the day.'

'That's awful, but we've been expecting it,' replied Denise, trying to keep the emotion out of her voice.

'I think it would be best to come over away, to see him before he goes.'

'I'll be there straight away.'

'Oh. Just one other thing, he insists that he must see Esther before he goes.'

Denise phoned her daughter straight away and they met at the hospital one hour later. As they sat either side of the patient, both

128

were holding back the tears. Philip James looked bad, the colour had gone from his face, his eyes looked sad as he struggled to breath.

'Esther,' he whispered, 'come here,'

She leant over and he said, 'find Nick Allen. Tell him his wife was murdered.'

'Where will I find him?' she replied.

'Try Sallys.'

Slowly he looked over Esther's shoulder towards the ward door. There he saw a black hooded figure slowly walking towards him. When he reached Philip's bed he stood silently at the end.

He looked at the figure and asked, 'is it time?'

The figure nodded.

Philip turned towards Denise and Esther and with a smile said 'goodbye.'

*

2022

PC Esther Robinson now Barnett, after her marriage to Steve, sits next to her partner PC Chris Straw, bored to tears in their patrol car. After her grandfather died, she gave up her job as an accountant and applied to join the police. She first met her partner whilst on her 22 weeks initial training course at Wymondham Training College in Norfolk. Chris is of medium height and build with a full head of hair and beard.

'I'm bored, bored, bored,' moaned Esther, putting another handful of *Haribos* into her mouth.

Chris gave a sigh; he'd heard it all before.

'Twelve fucking years and I'm still a PC. How many times have I applied to CID? Go on tell me.'

Shaking his head, Chris replied, 'I've lost count, do tell me.'

'I can't remember either, I've also lost count. But just tell me why, that's all I ask.'

'You know why, I've told you enough times.'

'I need to hear it just one more, and if I don't like it, I'm going to chuck it all in and go back to being an accountant.'

'No, you won't, you say that every time. You love your job, "it's your destiny, young Esther" imitating the Emperor from Star Wars.'

'Okay, but pretend you're the boss, and give me one good reason why I shouldn't be accepted for the CID.'

'Okay,' replied Chris. 'A bit of role-play then.'

'Go for it.'

'Esther, how many times have you been suspended in the last ten years.'

'I believe it is twice….but.'

Chris lifts his hand to stop her. 'And how many times have you been reprimanded?'

Esther drops her chin, then says 'but how many commendations have I had?'

'I believe it's three, and that's the only reason you're still in a job and just a PC.'

Esther sighed, 'that can't be the only reason, there are loads of examples where cops break the rules and still get promotion. For example, DI John Rebus and DI John Carlyle.'

'They're not real, they're fiction. It's not like that in the real world.' He looks at Esther, 'except in your case.'

Esther smiled, 'okay; but while you're being honest, is there anything else?'

'Just one more thing, and don't take it the wrong way. You're just too beautiful to be a detective, no-one would take you seriously.'

Esther offers the bag of *Haribos* to Chris, he pulls out a bear and a ring then says in a squeaky voice, 'maybe the bear could steal the ring, which is the crown jewels and run away with it, and maybe the police can find them.'

Esther, in a high voice replies, 'we are the police.'

The radio crackles and a voice says, 'control to Alpha Two Zero, are you anywhere in the vicinity of the High Street, robbery taking place in Patels Mini-Market'.

Esther replies 'control, just around the corner. We're on our way.'

As they pull up outside the mini market a small crowd has assemble, an old lady with her shopping trolly rushes up to them, 'I was in there, he let me go. He's got a gun.'

'Christ, that's all we need, I'll call in for armed response,' replied Chris. He looks round, just in time to see Esther walk into

130

the shop. 'No,' he screams, but it's too late, she disappears through the door.

Esther walks slowly towards the counter. She sees Mr Patel with his hands in the air. A tall man (she assumes it's a man) wearing dirty jeans, white trainers and a grey hoodie is pointing a pistol at Mr Patel, screaming at him to open the till. Mr Patel is silent, looking nervous and shaking his head. He spots Esther, she puts a finger to her lips, but it is too late and the robber senses something is wrong and turns around. Outraged, he storms towards Esther with his gun pointed at her forehead. She stands still. The gun is just a couple of inches away from her. What happened next can only be described by Chris who has entered the shop and watching from an unseen position.

'I had entered the shop without being seen and crept down another aisle so I could get a better look. I was terrified that if the gunman saw me, he would panic and shoot someone, but I couldn't leave Esther on her own. She looked so calm and if I'd blinked, I would have missed what happened next. In a flash Esther's left hand hit the gun whist the right hand smashed into his wrist. The gun went flying and his trigger finger was broken. Then with lightning speed she kicked him between the legs, as he bent forward her knee came up and smashed into his nose. As he hit the ground, she turned him over and cuffed him; all over in five seconds. The crowd outside were clapping wildly and cheering.'

Esther stood there looking pleased with herself, she saw Chis and said, 'another commendation, I think. Have you called it in?' Chris was about to pick the culprit up when Esther said, 'just one more thing,' and gave him a hard kick in the ribs.

'Better now?' asked Chris.

As they escorted the prisoner out, the armed response team arrived. Chris approached them and said,' suspect arrested, been told his rights, PC Barnett has the pistol in an evidence bag, no casualties.'

As their shift was nearly over, they took a slow drive back to the station.

'You're quiet,' said Esther, eating the last of her *haribos*.

131

'What the fuck were you doing back there, you could have got yourself killed.'

'Don't be such I drama queen, it wasn't even a real gun.'

'You weren't to know that and where the fuck did you learn how to disarm that bloke?'

'Oh, I had some self-defence classes a few years back.'

Chris thought for a while before saying, 'I remember back in training college, can't remember his name. You know, the one who kept harassing you. Had a tenner bet with most of the other cadets that he'll get inside your knickers before the end of the course.'

Esther shrugged her shoulders, 'vaguely remember something like that.'

'Mysteriously quit the course, I heard later that both arms were broken and every single finger on each hand.'

'I heard he fell down some stairs,' replied Esther with a smirk on her face. 'Do you think I'll get another commendation?'

Chris sighed, 'I expect so, but you'll definitely get a bollocking for not following protocols.'

'Couldn't give a toss, I've got two weeks holiday starting next week, so I can forget all about the job, and when I come back, I'll apply to join the CID again.'

What Chris didn't know and not many others did either was that Esther was a 2nd Dan in Shotokan and studied other fighting techniques such as Taekwondo, Kung fu and Jujitsu plus advance self-defence classes in United Krav Maga Defence Tactics. When she was single, even now she was married, she told her friends she was attending either keep fit, aerobics, or Pilates classes.

*

Saturday

'I don't believe it,' exclaimed Esther.

What's with the Victor Meldrew impression?' replied her husband, Steve.

Esther and Steve were sorting out the contents of her parents' bungalow that she had just inherited after the death of her stepfather six weeks ago. Being an only child, the will, which was recently read, was straight forward. Her mother died two years ago therefore she inherited the lot. Her mother's sister, Auntie Marion, had died many years ago. Apparently, she mixed with an unsavoury crowd and died of an drugs overdose. She was just 26 years old. Being fed up living in Norfolk, they decided that they would sell the bungalow, sell their house, and move nearer to London. Esther met Steve when she was working at the same accountancy firm. Perhaps, she could get transferred to the Met., where her talents would be more appreciated.

What have you found?' asked Steve, as he rummaged through a box containing Toby Jugs neatly wrapped in old newspaper. 'Who collects these things,' he muttered to himself.

'My granddad's old diaries, some date back to the sixties,' replied Esther.

'Just chuck them, no one's interested in old diaries.'

'I don't believe it.'

'Not again.'

'You are definitely not going to believe this. Do you remember what I told you what my granddad said on his deathbed: you know his last words to me?'

Remind me,' replied Steve as he unwrapped a Royal Daulton character jug of Henry VIII, and thinking *this may be worth a few bob.*

'He looked straight at me and with a tear in his eye said "find Nick Allen and tell him she was murdered" or something like that and I said where will I find him? He replied, "in Sallys". Then he was gone. I'd forgotten all about it. I've let him down.

Looking over at Esther and seeing that she was upset, he asked 'what has that got to do with the diaries?'

'I didn't take much notice at the time, because he was suffering from dementia, I thought he was just rambling.'

'So, what have you found?'

Esther took a deep breath and answered, 'I've just opened this diary from 1964, and I can't believe what I've found.'

Sunday 13 September 1964
It was supposed to be my day off and I was spending a pleasant afternoon in the garden when I received a call from the station. I was to phone Nick Allen on this number. Apparently, he and his friends have found the body of a boy

that had been missing for 5 years. How can a 14-year-old crack a case we've been unable to solve.

Steve took a sharp intake of breath, then said, 'that must be the same Nick Allen he mentioned.'

'Exactly. I wonder if there is any mention of *Sally's*' as she frantically turned the pages. It didn't take long to find what she was looking for. 'I've found it.'

Wednesday 16 September 1964
I needed to find Nick and his friends, and I knew exactly where they would be and at what time. I was right: in *Sally's Inn* after school and the boys did look worried. As they should be after beating that Catholic priest half to death. Still, after all the disgusting things he did, he deserved it.

Esther smiles, 'I'm getting to like this, Nick Allen.'

'So, what are you going to do now?' asked Steve, with a slightly worried look on his face.

'Need you ask,' replied Esther. 'Find this Nick Allen, assuming he's still alive. Find out who was murdered, then with or without his help solve the murder. Then I'll go to my boss and if they don't let me join the CID I'll quit and start up my own detective agency, just like Cormoran Strike. I'll get some business cards printed – **Esther Barnett, Private Investigator.**

'So how do you intend to find this Nick Allen?' asked Steve with a worried expression on his face.

'Well, I've got two weeks off, I reckon I'll have it cracked by the end of my holiday. First, I'll google Nick Allen; he may be famous or well known. I know my granddad was working at St. Albans in the sixties; I have a friend there. If she can get hold of the case file and get me a copy, that would be a good start.

That evening Esther sat down at her desk, computer turn on, notebook at the ready. First, she Googled Nick Allen + St. Albans, there was lots of stuff. Photos of him, books he has had published, his interest in London Pubs. She then checked his Facebook page. This was very revealing; he is a widower. Digging deeper she finds a post on the anniversary of his wife's death. She then did a detailed search on the death of Jane Allen, in which a local paper reveal that she died in a following a mysterious car crash. The coroner concluded that Jane died following a car crash in which no one else was involved. Accidental death.

The next step was to contact an acquaintance, Margret Jarvis in St. Albans, and ask her to look out the case notes for the crash. Further research revealed the *Sally's Inn* was now a Greek restaurant. After phoning Margret, explaining the case, and asking if she could stay with her for a few days whilst she started her investigation. Margret was overjoyed at the prospect of spending time with her old friend and stated that her husband Tony was away for a few nights up north, attending an antiques fair.

Sunday

Sunday morning Esther, dressed in her ME+EM jeans, Reiss blazer over a white silk camisole with a Mulberry handbag pulling her Lulu Guinness suitcase caught the 10.03 train from Norwich to London Liverpool Street. From there she took the underground to Farringdon where she caught the next train to St. Albans. Margret lived in a large semi-detached property in Hatfield Road, just a short taxi drive away.

Margret, an ex-dance teacher, who joined the force after a bad accident which restricted her ability to dance, was ecstatic when Esther arrived. After spending at least two hours reminiscing and knocking back two bottles of New Zealand Sauvignon Blanc, and they discussed the case. Esther explained about her discovery in her grandfather's diaries and his dying words. Margret stated that she had managed to get hold of the case files, which had not been put on the computer yet. She also said that Jim Constable, the records officer was a bit suspicious of her looking up such an old case.

'What did you say?' asked Esther, not wanting to get her friend into trouble.

Margret replied, 'just looking at old cases for my sergeant's exam.'

'Did he believe you?'

Margret just shrugged her shoulders.

'Okay, have you had a look at them, yet?'

'I have, and your suspicions are right. There is something dodgy about the whole thing.'

'Such as?' replied Esther, getting excited.

'Well for a start, they are not very thorough, the coroner stated that Jane Allen died of 'accidental death, due to drink driving.' It was 10 o'clock in the morning, for fucks sake. One witness, Christopher Vincent, who was jogging at the time, saw the car lose control: veer off the road, straight into a tree. He called 999 on his mobile, then rushed to the scene of the accident but couldn't get to Jane because the door was stuck. He never attended the hearing, basic report from the garage stated that they could find nothing wrong with the car, brakes, tyres, and steering all looked okay. She was driving the family car, a red Renault Laguna.'

'Interesting, but it all seems a bit vague.'

'Yeah, but why did your grandfather think it was murder?'

'No idea, but I'm still going to investigate it. I'll start tomorrow. I'm in no state to start investigating around today. I'll start with the witness.'

'No, we'll start tomorrow, I've booked a week off; do you really think I would miss this? If you're investigating, it's not going to be without some excitement. And remember what the book says, "The modern-day approach to murder recognises the fact that there is no longer the place for the "lone entrepreneur" investigating officer", and you'll need a driver.'

*

Monday

At 10.00am the next morning Esther and Margret were knocking on the front door of Chistopher Vincent's house in Sandpit Lane; the only witness to the accident. The door was answered by an attractive woman in her mid-fifties.

'Good morning, can I help you?' she asked, with a half-smile on her face.

'Good morning,' replied Margret. 'I'm PC Jarvis and this is PC Barnett,' showing her warrant card. 'We were just wondering if you husband Christopher was in. We would like to ask him a few questions.

'Is this a joke? Are you really the police, why aren't you in uniform?'

Esther stepped forward and with a warming smile replied, 'It's a long story but we are police officers, and we are doing some private investigating on an old case that is very personal to me. We were just hoping he could clarify a few details about a car accident that he witnessed about 20 years ago.'

The lady looked stunned for a few minutes, the said, 'you better come in.'

Esther and Margret followed the lady in the nicely decorated conservatory.

'Would you like some tea or coffee, I've a feeling this is going to take some time, by the way, my name is Judith, and I'm Chistopher's widow.'

With the coffee served along with a plate of Chocolate Digestives, dark chocolate, Esther's favourite, Judith started to speak. 'My husband died one week after the accident; hit and run. He always went for a jog in the morning before breakfast. He always ran along Cooper's Green Lane, that was where the accident took place. I remember the day like it was yesterday, he was in a right state when he came home. He tried to save the woman, but he couldn't open the car door. He phoned 999, but when they arrived and opened the door, she was gone.'

'Did he mention what exactly happened?' asked Esther.

'Oh yes, he wrote it all down while it was fresh in his mind. He was very conscientious, wrote everything down.'

'Do you remember what happened?'

'As far as I can remember a red car with the lady driving, was overtaken by a black BMW that swerved in front of it, causing the red car off the road and hit a tree.'

'So,' Esther's mind was racing. 'He gave his statement at the scene; did they follow it up. Come to the house, make a formal statement for him to sign?'

'No, but as I said, he was killed a week later.'

Margret could tell that Judith was getting a little upset but asked. 'If it's not too much, could you tell us a bit about the hit and run.'

'Not much to tell really, no witnesses, another jogger found him by the side of the road. He called an ambulance, but he was already dead.'

'I'm so sorry, that must have been awful for you.'

It still hurts, but they say time is a great healer. Never got married again, had a few lovers but it never seemed right. Then I started batting for the other side. In a nice relationship with a girl named Maria, sounds funny. "I've just met a girl called Maria". Doesn't seem like I'm betraying Christopher.' Doesn't shock you, does it?'

'Of course not,' said Esther and Margret in unison.

'Do you still have what he wrote down?' asked Esther.

'I expect so, I never got round to throwing any of Christopher's stuff away. It might take a while to find it. If you give me your mobile number, I'll call you if I find it.'

'That will be great,' replied Esther, 'and you're sure it was a BMW.'

'Absolutely, I hate BMW's. Not so much the cars but their drivers. It's not their fault; did you know that the Germans Hex the cars.'

'What does that mean?' asked Margret.

'You're obviously not a Harry Potter fan,' replied Esther. 'It means to put a curse on someone or something.'

Judith beaming said, 'that's right, they put a hex on all the cars they send to Britain which turns all the drivers into boy-racers. You are driving along the road at 30mph in a 30 mile an hour zone then you notice a BMW behind you, and all the time they are trying to overtake. You watch them in your rear-view mirror, and they are edging out just waiting to overtake. And signalling, don't get me started on signalling. Do they even know the car has indicators? And they are a nightmare at roundabouts, never in the right lane. Have you noticed that the majority of accidents on the M25 involve a BMW. And did you know that when they get points put on their licence, they think it's a reward from the police for good driving. Okay, that's my rant for the day.'

Esther and Margret couldn't stop laughing.

Esther said, 'there could be some truth in that.'

'Is there anything else, don't get me wrong. It's nice talking to you but I have a Pilates class in thirty minutes,'

Esther and Margret stood up and Esther replied 'I think that's all for the moment. You've given us something to work on but let us know if you find that note.'

Esther and Margret sat in the car. Margret asked 'What do you reckon, what have we learned?

Esther sighed, 'Well she was definitely murdered and there was a cover-up. But what worries me is the death of Christopher. A week after he saw the accident he's killed. I think he was silenced.'

'So, it looks like we are searching for a serial killer,' replied Margret.

'And he's a cop.'

It was almost noon, so the girls decided to have lunch at the *Speckled Hen* pub in Hatfield Road. Formally known as the *Bunch of Cherries* the current building was erected in 1963 and was sold to *Green King* in 2005. Esther ordered Scampi and Chips with tartare sauce and garden peas and a glass of Sauvignon Blanc. Margret settled for Battered Halloumi and Chips with Mushy peas and a glass of orange juice.

'So, what's our next move?' asked Margret.

'Two things, first I would like to see the report on the hit and run and two, visit the garage where the car was taken.'

'Okay, I'll pop back to the station this afternoon and see what I can find.'

'Won't they think it suspicious you are lurking around the station when you supposed to be on holiday?'

Margret frowned, 'I'm a woman, I'm almost invisible, no one will even notice me. If they do, I'll say I'm still doing research for my Sargent's exam.'

'Okay, but I don't want you to get into any trouble.'

''I'll be fine, look I tell you what we'll do. We'll take my car home and then get the bus into town. While I go to the station you can have a look round St. Albans town centre, then we'll go for a drink.'

Esther thought then replied, 'I'd like to visit the Mermaid, is that near the town centre? From my research about Nick Allen, that's a regular haunt of his.'

Margret smiled, 'that's where I was going to suggest, it's got a lovely garden.'

After dropping the car back at Margret's, they caught the UNO 601 bus and alighted opposite the Alban City school at the top of Hatfield Road. Esther had made a few notes on the places she wanted to visit. First was *Sallys Coffee Bar*, she knew it was closed ages ago and was now a Greek restaurant called *Anastasias.* Standing on the opposite side of the road, looking at it and trying to imagine her grandfather talking to the young Nick Allen and his friends back in the sixties. After a leisurely stroll through the town centre, she found herself outside *The Boot* public house. Built in 1420 it is one of the oldest pubs in the UK. The story goes that soldiers were drinking in this pub in 1455 when the 1st Battle of St. Albans started. Apparently, it took about 20 minutes for the soldiers to put on their armour, by which time the battle was over. She the crossed the road, ventured down Waxhouse gate to have a look at the Cathedral. Promising herself that one day she would come back and explore the inside of the Cathedral. She then made her way up George Street, spending more time than she should window shopping. Hoping that she wouldn't be late meeting Margret, she walked briskly to the *Mermaid* public house.

The Mermaid pub dates from the 19th century when it was surrounded by fields. It was an "ale house" mainly for farm workers but, observing the social graces of the time, it had two bars that enabled the better-off to avoid men in working clothes. As luck would have it, she bumped into Margret as she crossed Upper Marlborough Road, and they made their way to the pub together. Inside they were greeted by a pretty barmaid dressed simply in plain white t-shirt and blue jeans. When asked her name she replied 'Ella'. They ordered a bottle of Pinot Grigio and two glasses of tap water with ice and lemon.

'Haven't seen you in here before,' said Ella, in a friendly manner.

'No, it's my first time, I'm down here from Norfolk to visit my friend,' replied Esther.

'Ah that's nice. Should have known from the accent.'

'God is it that noticeable,' laughed Esther.

'No, it's not that bad, I've heard worse.'

'Good, look can I ask you a question?'

'Certainly.'

'Do you know someone that drinks in here called, Nick Allen.'

'Are you related to him?'

Esther looked surprised, 'why did you ask that?'

'Nothing, just wondering. Yes, lovely man, he's a regular.'

'When would be the best time to catch him?'

'It varies, but he's always here on Wednesday nights for the music. It's the *Beatniks* this week, they're great, you don't want to miss them. But get here early if you want to get a seat. He comes here with a few mates. If you want to catch him on his own, Friday afternoon is your best bet. He comes in here about three and spends an hour on his own reading before his friends turn up.'

'Thank you, you've been very helpful.'

'Are you sure you're not related?'

'Why do you keep asking that?' But Ella had moved away to serve another customer.

Taking their drinks into garden and finding a nice table in the shade, Esther was anxious to know what Margret had found.

'I found the case notes quite easily, they haven't put them on the computer yet. Not much to say. Christopher was hit by an unknown driver and left to die. Found by a jogger called Keith Wells who dialled 999 and tried CPR, but with no result.'

'I think we need to interview him, have you got an address,' asked Esther.

'I have, let's hope he hasn't moved.'

They sat there for a while, without speaking, enjoying the warmth and quiet. Then Esther asked, 'did anyone see you at the station?'

'No one took any notice of me, not even a hello, except for Jim again. He nodded but looked curious.'

'Let's hope you don't have to go there again; we don't want anyone getting suspicious.'

Esther was in deep thought, then asked, 'what was there a name of the investigating officer?'

'Good question, I wrote it done; yes, it was DC Robert Mills.'

'Wasn't that the same person whose name was on the other report?'

Margret took a deep intake of breath then said, 'you're right; looks like we have a suspect.'

'Is he still on the force,' replied Esther excitedly.

'He is, due for retirement very soon, he's a DS now. They call him Teflon Mills, he's bent as a nine-bob note, but nothing sticks.'

'Do you think he's capable of murder?'

'Not sure he would do it himself, but he could definitely get someone else to do it.'

'Tomorrow we'll interview Keith Wells, I suggest you go in uniform. I didn't bring mine. So, I'll pretend to be CID, save explaining it all again.'

*

Tuesday

Keith Wells lived in a one-bedroom maisonette in Newgate Close, not too far from Margret's home. At 10.00am Margret, in uniform, and Esther were ringing his doorbell. After a few minutes the door was opened by a scruffy looking man in his early sixties wearing a dirty white t-shirt, faded blue jeans and nothing on his feet. His grey hair was tied back in a ponytail, unshaven, with a unkept moustache and soul patch.

Looking surprised at his visitors he said 'Ding, dong, what have we got here? It's a long time since two beauties appeared on my doorstep so early in the morning. What do I owe the pleasure?'

Esther stepped forward and quickly flashing her warrant card said, 'my name is DC Esther Barnett, and this is PC Margret Jarvis, may we come in and ask you a few questions.'

'By all means, come in, come in, ask me anything you like.'

Keith led them through to the lounge, which was reasonably clean, but there was an unusual smell which Esther recognised as Cannabis. When they were seated Esther asked if he would open the window.

'Ah', said Keith. 'Is that why you called, I only use it for medicinal purposes. Arthritis, it will be the death of me,'

'If the weed doesn't get you first,' replied Margret, sarcastically.

Esther continued, 'No, we are not here about your habit, we'll let the Drugs Squad deal with that.'

Keith looked terrified.

'Just kidding, we'll let you slowly kill yourself. No, we want to ask you a few questions about an incident that happened a few years back. Sorry, I forgot to ask, are you Keith Wells?'

'Of course I am, now what incident are we referring to?'

'In 2003 you were jogging along Coopers Green Lane, when you found another jogger, lying by the side of the road. Can you tell us in your own words about this incident.'

Keith looked pensive, then said, 'can I get you a tea, coffee, beer, wine or would you like a smoke, just joking.'

Esther raised her eyebrows, 'we don't want any of those things, we're Jehovah Witnesses…, just kidding. Please, just tell what happened.'

'Right, I was jogging down Coopers Green Lane, away from St. Albans. I was on the right-hand side, facing the oncoming traffic. I was taught that at cubs. Then I saw someone lying by the side of the road on the other side. I didn't know him. What was his name?'

'Christopher,' replied Margret, 'carry on.'

'As I said, I didn't know him, but saw him often. He was always running towards me on the opposite side of the road.'

'Must have gone to the same cub group,' said Margret, straight-faced.

Keith just shook his head, then continued. 'I rushed over to him, he wasn't breathing, I tried CPR, but it was clear he was dead. Luckily, I had my mobile on and as you lot say – I called it in, really freaked me out, had to take a month off work. Cost me a fortune in therapy.'

'That must have been awful for you, are you okay now?' Asked Margret in a condescending way.

'Yes, I think so, thank you for asking.'

Esther, trying not to laugh asked, 'is there anything else you can add. Did you see any other cars on the road?'

'Well actually there was, as I said in my statement about five minutes before, a black BMW came towards and nearly hit me.' Keith paused, then continued. 'Nothing else I can think off.'

Esther looked at Margret and she nodded. 'I think that will be all, thank you for your time.'

'Are you sure you won't stay for a drink, I don't get many visitors,' asked Keith.

Esther and Margret stood up and Esther said, 'another time, sorry but we have a full schedule today. Catching killers is a full-time job.'

Once outside Margret asked, 'what did you make of him?'

Esther smiled and replied, 'you know what they say, under every ponytail there is an arsehole.'

They drove back to Margret's house so that she could change back into her civies.

'What's the plan for the rest of the day?' Asked Esther.

'Well, I need to do some shopping. So, we'll pop up the Quadrant then I'll take you to lunch at the Queens Head in Sandridge. After that we need to see the garage that examined the car after the crash. It's a long time ago but they may still have records.'

'Good plan, but unless the actual mechanic is still there it will be a waste of time, because the records will be the same as the one, we already have.'

'You never know, look we've only been at for one day and we have a suspect already. I've got a feeling at this rate; we'll have the case closed by Friday.'

Esther smiled, 'of course you're right, but I haven't smacked anyone yet and that's the best part.'

Margret chuckled, 'So when was the last time you smacked someone in the line of duty?'

'Actually, only last week; some nut-job tried to rob a mini-market with a fake gun. I disarmed him and gave him a good smack.'

'And you wonder why you've never got promoted.'

There has been a Queens Head on this site from at least 1763, as attested by the minutes of a parish meeting held there. Exactly who the Queen was in question is debatable. A strong candidate, apart from the likeness of the image would be Elizabeth 1st. Princess Elizabeth was shielded by the Thrale family in Nomansland, a mere mile or so away when she was in hiding from Queen Mary. A grateful Elizabeth bestowed family arms on the Thrale family when she became Queen. The Queen's Head is one of three pubs in the village of Sandridge.

'This is nice,' said Esther as the parked the car and walked towards the pub.

'It's one of my favourites, I sometimes come here on Sundays with Tony, they do a cracking Sunday Lunch.'

After checking out the menu, Esther chose Ham, egg and chips and a half pint of cider, whilst Margret ordered Caesar Salad and a J2O, orange and passion fruit. Although the pub was quite busy, they managed to grab a table. Esther noticed that a few of the older drinkers who looked like regulars kept staring at her.

'Am I imagining it or those two at the bar giving us the eye?'

'If they are, they're a bit old for my taste, but I think that they may have never seen anyone as beautiful as you in this pub before.'

'I expect your right, after all they are only human.'

When they had finished their meal Esther went to the bar to order coffees. One of the old men who had been eyeing Esther said, 'sorry if I keep staring, but do I know you? You look familiar.'

'I doubt it,' replied Esther, 'it's my first time in this pub and I've only been in St. Albans two days.'

'Well then, I apologise for staring, but it's nice to meet you, and my names Peter, Peter Parfitt, village poacher. If you want a rabbit or a pheasant, I'm your man.'

'Thank you,' replied Esther. 'I'm partial to a bit of game. My names Esther and I'm a police officer.'

'Oh Shit,' replied Peter. 'Should have kept my mouth shut.'

Esther laughed, 'It's alright, I'm not from round here, and I have my own poachers back home to supply me, but it's nice to meet you.

Esther went back to her seat with a big smile on her face.

Suitably refreshed they decided to drive to Welwyn Garden City Police Headquarters to check out the garage.

They were greeted by a pleasant mechanic who introduced himself as Dave Winch. Dave was in his sixties, short with grey hair and a friendly face.

'Afternoon ladies how can I help you?' asked Dave.

'We're looking for the records of an accident that happened in 2003,' replied Margret.

'Give me a few minutes and I'll see if I can find them.'

Dave returned five minutes later with a folder, and it didn't take long to find what they were looking for.

Each report was in a plastic sleeve.

'Who did the inspection, and does he still work here?' asked Esther.

'Let me look, oh it was Ray Timberlake. No, he does work here anymore.'

'Is there something you want to tell us?' asked Margret, sensing Dave was holding something back.

'Well, I remember this one, because Ray left a week after and then emigrated to Australia. I was always suspicious because we were good mates, but I've never heard from him since.'

Margret looked closer, 'it's the same as the one we've got; nothing wrong with the car.'

'Just a minute,' said Esther, noticing a staple in the top corner.

Dave pulled out the report and found an envelope attached at the back. He pulled it off and handed it to Esther. In the envelope was a handwritten letter; Esther read it out.

To whoever is reading this you must have worked out that the report has been altered. For that I'm eternally sorry. But you must realise that it was not done willingly. I was in no position to refuse. Let me explain. I was in trouble; my gambling was out of control, and I owed a lot of money to some not very nice people. I received a phone call offering me a way out. They said they would pay off my debts and give me an extra £1000 if I falsified the report and disappeared. We had always talked about emigrating to Australia. So, we sold our house, moved up north and, rented a cheap property until all the paperwork was sorted. We are settled here down under, and we have a good life. But I'm always looking over my shoulder just waiting for that dreaded day. Please don't think bad of me. Just for the record the brakes and airbag had been tampered with.

All three just stood there looking at each other before Dave said, 'well that's a turn up for the book. What happens now?'

'We'll take the letter, it's a crucial part of our investigation,' replied Margret.

The girls said their goodbyes, made their way to car and drove home.

*

Wednesday

With nothing planned for the morning the girls decided to have a lazy one. Margret's husband Tony had left early on an antique buying trip. Margret had showered, and dressed in her onesie was in the kitchen making coffee and toast. Esther was in the bathroom, sitting on the toilet when she heard the doorbell go. *Wonder who that is* she thought. Then she heard a shuffle which was followed by a scream. She quietly made her way downstairs and sensed the intruders were in the living room. Opening the door, she was not happy with what she saw. Margret was sitting in the armchair sporting a red mark on her cheek. Hovering over were two thugs, both dressed all in black, trying to look hard.

'What have we here?' said the first thug who was about five nine, had short black hair and a five o'clock shadow. 'How about a kiss then.'

'No problem,' replied Esther. 'Come and get it.'

Thug number one walked closer to Esther and received his kiss. Only it wasn't what he expected; he received a Glasgow Kiss – a sudden headbutt to the nose, followed by a kick to the groin. As he fell to the floor, Esther stamped on his knee. The second thug, a bit taller than his mate rushed at Esther, but was felled with a right to the jaw.

Esther turned to Margret, 'are you alright?' she asked.

Margret nodded.

'Okay, we need to tie these to us, have you any duct tape?'

'Yes, in the kitchen, I'll get it.'

When she returned, they quickly tied them up.

'What do we do now?' asked Margret.

'We need them to tell us who hired them. If they don't talk, we'll torture them. Let's hope they don't talk,' replied Esther, smiling.

'I need to go to hospital, you've broken my knee,' cried the thug number one.

'Just tell us who sent you.'

'We don't know.'

'Not good enough.' Esther sighed, 'what method shall we use? '

Margret just shook her head and wondered if Esther was capable of torturing someone. She had a nasty feeling that she was.

'What would Lisbeth Salander do, shame we haven't got a tattooing machine. We could do what she did in the film, stick a large object up their arse. A rolling pin would do, but you wouldn't want to roll your pastry with it afterwards. I know, we'll use your kitchen blow torch on the soles of their feet. That should make the talk. You take their shoes and socks off and I'll get it from the kitchen.'

'You're bluffing, you wouldn't dare torture us,' said thug two.

The scream was terrifying as Esther lit the torch and applied the flame to the sole of his foot. Esther looked at thug two, licking her lips.

'She's mad, we honestly don't know. We only communicate by phone; we're supposed to phone him when we've finished with you.'

Margret was getting worried now and said, 'look just tell why you are here.'

Thug two looked at thug one, thug one looked at Esther. Esther lit the blow torch, Thug two nodded.

'I'll tell you everything.'

'Go on I'm all ears,' said Esther.

'We're professional enforcers, we get information out of people who don't want to give the information, or like you, encourage people like you to stop interfering in things that don't concern you.'

'And that means knocking defenceless young women about?' asked Esther.

Both thugs had dropped their heads.

Esther said 'Margret, search them, let me see their wallets and phones.'

'Right,' taking thug one's phone, 'who do you phone?'

'It's the only number on there; it's a burner.'

'Okay, put it on speaker, call whoever and tell them the job is done.'

Thug number did it without question. Margret went through their wallets, removing all the bank notes and saying 'compensation'. She also made a note of their names and addresses.

'What happens now?' asked thug two.

'Did he tell you who I was?' asked Margret.

'No, we were told to rough you up a bit and tell you to keep your nose out of other people's business.'

'Did they mention that I was a police officer.'

Thug two looked at thug one, 'shit, they never mentioned that. So, what happens now? You can't turn us in after torturing us.'

Esther smiled, 'so you're not as dumb as you look. You're right, we'll let you go. But you don't say a word to your employer. Remember I know where you live, and I won't be so gentle next time.'

Margret untied them, and thug two helped thug one, who was struggling to walk out of the house to their car – a black BMW.

'That was fun,' said Esther, with a big smile on her face.

'Remind me never to get on the wrong side of you,' replied Margret.

'So, where does that leave us?' asked Esther.

'I recognised the voice, it's the same man who signed all those false reports – DS Roberts Mills.'

'That's good, now we know who did it and how he did it, we just need to know why and tonight we will find out when we meet this Nick Allen bloke.

Nick Allen, now seventy-two, a retired Maths lecturer was enjoying his 10th year of retirement. Tonight, the Wednesday Night Reborn club, which was formed during the COVID lockdown, were meeting at the *Mermaid* pub for the Wednesday music session featuring their favourite duo the *Beatniks*. The gang were all there, Nick was the last to arrive due to his bus being late. Neal was at the bar and asked Nick what he wanted to drink.

'Pint of Suffolk County please,'

'Coming right up,' replied Ella.

'Thanks mate,' said Nick. 'How are you today, no cold, gout, or COVID.

Neal laughed, 'are you saying I'm a hypochondriac?'

'Of course not, that's the only thing you don't suffer from.'

'I'm fine, although my back has been giving me jip.'

Ella came back with Nick's pint and said, 'there was a woman in here on Monday asking after you.'

'I wonder who that was, did she give a name?'

'No, but she asked when you were in, and I said you were always in for the music?'

Nick smiled, 'could be my lucky day.'

Picking up his pint they ventured outside to join the rest of his friends.

'Are you ready yet?' shouted Margret.

'Coming,' replied Esther as she came down the stairs. She hadn't overdressed for the evening, new looking jeans, plain cream blouse, and a yellow cashmere jumper tied around her neck. Sunglasses, gold chain and two-inch heels. Margret stuck to her usual style, short black skirt over black tights, a black lacy blouse, and a black shawl.

They arrived at the pub just a few minutes after Nick had joined his friends, and were served by a very pretty, well-built barmaid called Grace. Esther ordered a bottle of Prosecco and two glasses of tap water with ice and lemon. After paying, Grace asked, 'do I know you, you look familiar?'

'I don't think so,' replied Esther. Then turning to Margret, 'what is it with this place?'

They made their way outside and found a seat with a good view of the stage.

'It's funny,' said Esther, 'all the songs they are playing are from the 60s, Beatles, Stones, the Who, and I know all the words, and I wasn't even born then.'

'I know, but they are bloody good. I'm really enjoying myself. It must have been great growing up then.'

The duo announced that they would be taking a break after this next number *All or Nothing* by the *Small Faces.*

When the song was finished Esther and Margret made their way back inside and found an empty table out of the way by the dart board.

'How are we going to play this?' asked Margret.

'Just go outside and tell him someone wants to speak to him urgently.'

'So, he's here then, you've seen him?'

'Oh yes, he's with his mates on a table near the entrance to the pub. You'll recognise him, not bad looking for his age. Silver hair, glasses, and a black Beatles t-shirt.'

The Wednesday Night Reborn Club were in deep conversation when Margret approached their table.

'Look, it's Morticia coming to join us,' said Neal.

Margret ignored the remark and spoke directly to Nick. 'I believe you are Nick Allen, and my friend wants to talk to you on an urgent matter, follow me please.'

Nick looked at his friends, shrugged his shoulders and followed Margret into the pub. When he set eyes on Esther, he was set back for a moment thinking that it was his daughter Sarah. Same short blonde hair, blue eyes, very good looking. But, on a second look, she was taller, broader and a bit more muscular.

Esther stood up and offered her hand, 'my name is Esther Barnett, and this is my friend Margret Jarvis. And we are here to help you find out who killed your wife.'

Nick was stunned and was lost for words.

'Oh,' she added 'and we are police officers.'

Margret looked at Esther and replied, 'you could have broken it to him a bit easier.'

'Nah, I don't Pussyfoot around, tell it to them straight. I don't think our friend here minds.'

Nick was nonplussed, but managed to say, 'I think you'd better start at the beginning.'

'Good idea,' said Esther, 'well as I said, my name is Esther and I'm the granddaughter of DCI James Phillips whom I believe you once knew.'

This hit Nick like a punch in the stomach as all those memories of yesteryear came flooding back.

All Nick could manage was, 'how is he?'

'Unfortunately, he died in 2010.'

Nick was feeling very emotional and could feel a tear running down his cheek.

Esther could see that Nick was upset, so tried to lighten the mood, 'he thought the world of you, all your adventures with him.'

Nick chuckled, 'we certainly made his life more interesting. Now tell me, what makes you think my wife was murdered?'

Margret chipped in, 'best you start from the very beginning.'

Esther went on to explain about her grandfather's last words and how she found your name in his old diaries. She also explained what they had found out so far.

'That's very interesting, but how did he know she was murdered?' asked Nick. 'I mean its years since I last saw him, and he must have retired by the time of the accident.'

'That's the mystery, but it seems it's true and we have a suspect. It's a bent copper called Robert Mills; do you know him?'

'Never heard of him.' Nick was thinking hard, 'I have a theory, but it's a bit far-fetched.'

'Let's hear it,' asked Esther, getting excited.

Nick replied, 'as Sherlock Holmes would say "insensibly one begins to twist the facts to suit theories, instead of theories to suit the facts," or something like that. We need to do a thorough background check on Robert Mills, from the moment he was born, parents, distant relations, the works, and I know just the man for the job. A man called Gary Broadbent, he's good at genealogy, and other stuff, and I think he is here tonight.'

Margret butted in, 'I know him quite well, I'll go and find him.'

'So,' said Esther, turning to Nick, 'I read that you're a bit of a trouble-shooter?'

Nick laughed, 'that was a long time ago, so tell me about yourself and why you want to solve this murder.'

'It was my grandfather's dying words and I feel guilty that I have let him down. I had totally forgotten what he had said until I read his diaries. On a personal level, if I solve this it might give me a chance to join the CID.'

Before Esther could continue, Margret had returned with Gary Broadbent, a slim gentleman in his late 50s. They sat down and Nick explained what they wanted. Gary seemed excited and told them to be here on Friday at 2.00pm and he'll have all the answers. In the background they could hear the music playing, the *Beatniks* starting their 2nd set. Gary got up said 'goodbye, see you Friday.'

'I expect you want to go back to your friends now?' said Esther, looking at Nick.

'I'm in no hurry.'

'What are doing tomorrow?' asked Esther.

'Why?'

'Well, from my research it seems you know a lot about London. So, I thought. If you were free, you could take me for a day out. I've never been to the Tower of London.'

Thursday

Esther and Nick had arranged to meet at the St Albans City station and take the train to London. Nick had purchased tickets to the Tower of London online, to save time. The Tower opened at 10.00am and the couple arrived soon after and spent the next three hours enjoying all that was on offer. They decided to visit the Crown Jewels first which took up the first hour. From there they visited the White Tower which includes St John's Chapel, and the historic armour Henry VIII, Charles I and James II in the line of Kings. As with any tour they ended up in the gift shop, where Nick bought Esther, a Beefeater Bear Soft Toy. Esther stated that she was feeling hungry and wanted to know where Nick was taking her for lunch. He said that he knew a very nice pub, not far away that dishes up very good food.

Leaving the Tower, they walked up Savage Gardens, then turned left into Crutched Friars where this classic pub the *Crutched Friar* was situated. Finding a nice table, they checked out the menu, Esthers choosing the Lamb Shank whist Nick ordered Hunter's Chicken. These were accompanied with a bottle of New Zealand Sauvignon Blanc.

Suitably refreshed Esther asked what was next for her to marvel at. Nick had it all planned, and they took a short walk to the Monument. The 202ft column, designed by Chritopher Wren and Dr. Robert Hooke, was built to commemorate the Great Fire of London of 1666, and stands on the piazza between Fish Street and Monument Street. Esther declined the offer to climb the 311 steps to the top, preferring to admire the construction from ground level. Esther had stated earlier that she didn't want to be too late home as she had planned to take Margret and Tony out tonight, a way of thanking them for putting her up. Nick said that he had one more important thing to show her. Leaving the Monument, they made their way towards London Bridge then stopped off at the Church of Saint Magnus-the-Martyr. Nick wanted to show Esther the famous 4 metre model of the old London Bridge. Created by David T. Aggett in 1987 who decided to create a scale model of the old bridge which captured in exquisite details, not only the bridge itself, but also the sheer frenetic confusion that must have emanated from the hundreds if not thousands of people who would have crossed the bridge, day in and day out, throughout its medieval existence. Time was getting on, so they made their way across London Bridge and caught the next train home.

Friday
Nick had just finished his bi-weekly over-50s men only keep-fit class when he was approached by his life-long friend Don Patrick.

'So, what was that all about Wednesday evening, you were very secretive and who were those two gorgeous ladies?' asked Don.

'Okay, if you really want to know, and you might not believe it, but they are WPCs and they are trying to find out who murdered Jane,' replied Nick.

'You can't call them WPCs any more they are just PCs.'

Nick raised his eyebrows; he was getting a little annoyed with Don now he has gone all woke.

'Okay, I repeat what I said just for you. They are Police Officers without penises, and they are trying to find out who killed my wife, is that better?'

'No need to be like that, I was just saying,' replied Don, a little upset.

I'm sorry, anyway, I'm meeting them this afternoon at the Mermaid and hopefully we will have solved the case.'

'Just like the old days; anything I can do?' replied Don, hoping he would say no.

'I think we're okay, we're meeting Gary Broadbent this afternoon, and hopefully he'll have the final piece to the jigsaw. Are you up there this afternoon?'

'Yes, I'll be there at 4.00.'

They had reached the carpark where they said goodbye, and they both drove home.

It was a glorious sunny afternoon when Nick entered the Mermaid and ordered a pint of Stowford Press cider. The garden was quite busy, and he spotted Esther and Margret already seating along with Gary Broadbent in a shady position. Gary stood up and shook Nick's hand before Nick greeted the girls with a kiss on the cheek. Always the gentleman. Nick noticed that the girls were both drinking cider whilst Gary had a pint of Citra.

'So, what have you got for us?' asked Nick.

'Oh, you are going to like this, it's very interesting,' beamed Gary. 'So, let's go back to when Robert Mills was born. He was born in St. Albans in 1960 and his name was …. Robert Higgens. His father is or was Danny Higgens.'

Nick jumped in, 'you say he was?'

'Oh definitely, he committed suicide whilst in prison, serving life for Patricide. That's killing your father. Whilst in prison Robert's mum divorced him, re-married and she and Robert took his new dad's name.'

Esther and Margret both looked at Nick, waiting for him to say something. Nick was miles away, almost in a trance. Esther gave him a shove and said, 'come on then, tell us all.'

Taking in a deep breath he looked at his companions and said, 'It all makes sense now.'

Esther could see that he was getting upset, so with an arm around the shoulder said, 'come on. Let's finish this and put the bastard away.'

Nick looked at Esther and said, 'I think you know the answers if you have read your grandfather's diaries.'

'It's coming together, but I need to hear it from you.'

155

'Okay, let's begin. Back in 1965, I along with my friends Don, who'll be here later, and Keith were part time Private Investigators. We solved people's problems and sometimes we were helped by your grandfather.'

Nick chuckled, 'and sometimes we helped him, although he would never admit it. At the beginning of '65 I was set up by person or persons unknown. I was arrested and charged with burglary. This led to me having to leave school and find a job. Also, all my friends deserted me; I almost had a breakdown. The only person who could help me clear my name was your grandfather, but I couldn't find him. As it happened, he also had been set up and suspended. By chance, one Sunday morning, after church, I bumped into him, and we put our heads together to find out who had set us both up. As it turned out it was a gangster from North London through one of his villains in St Albans. All the evidence pointed to Robert's grandfather who was Assistant Chief Commissioner at the time. When we went to arrest him, yes, I was there, Robert's dad shot his dad and made it look like suicide. He didn't make a very good job of hiding it and we soon worked out that he had murdered his dad. Therefore, I surmised that he killed Jane as revenge.' Then Nick thought, and said, 'I just remembered, on the day of the accident Jane had borrowed my car, as hers was in for a Service and MOT. The bastard was trying to kill me.'

The group were silent for a minute, before Gary said, 'I'm glad I was able to help, but I'll leave you to plan your next move.'

Nick stood up and shook Gary's hand and said, 'thanks mate, you've been a great help, let me buy you a beer. Girls, same again?'

With all the glasses replenished Nick, Esther and Margret sat in quiet, each deep in thought. Their calm was broken when Margret saw someone and said, 'I don't fucking believe it.'

'What is it,' asked Esther.

'Look who's just walked in with his mates…. Robert Mills.'

'How are we going to play this,' asked Margret, 'shall I just go over there and arrest him?'

'I think his mates would just laugh at you,' replied Esther.

'This is how we will play it. I'll go over and introduce myself, wind him up, and see what happens,' said Nick.

'You mean there might be a bit of violence,' smirked Esther, rubbing her hands together. 'Oh goody.'

Robert Mills was standing there with his mates, laughing, and joking, not a care in the world. At 62 years old, he was about to retire and was looking forward to a long carefree retirement.

'Excuse me Robert, could I have a quick word,' asked Nick.

Robert turned and looked at Nick, 'do I know you?'

Nick could feel his blood level rising but remained calm. 'I don't know, do you?'

'Sorry, what's this about, your face is not familiar.'

Nick shrugged his shoulders, 'maybe, but you know of me. After all you killed my wife. My name is Allen, Nick Allen.'

Robert went as white as a ghost and started breathing heavy. 'It wasn't me and you can't prove anything.'

'Oh, I think we can. We know that you altered all the case notes, had the only witness killed and sent two thugs to rough up PC Jarvis.'

'It wasn't me.'

'Come off it, it was you who answered the thug's phone, PC Jarvis recognised your voice'.

'It wasn't your wife that was meant to be killed, it was you.'

'I've already realised that; you're just another bent copper, just like your dad.'

The sweat was now pouring from Robert's forehead, 'my dad was a great copper and if you and that meddling DI hadn't fitted him up, he would still be alive today.'

'Perhaps you should say that to my friend over there, she's, his granddaughter.'

Esther gave a little wave.

'You framed my dad, my granddad committed suicide.'

Nick just smiled, 'no he didn't, he killed him in cold blood. I know I was there.' He knew what was going to happen next and was ready for it.

Robert took a swing at him, Nick raised his left arm to block and countered with a straight right to the nose, blood quickly flowed. Robert then rushed at Nick, who side stepped, and aimed a side kick to the knee. Robert fell to the floor screaming. No sooner had he hit the ground Robert's three mates came rushing at Nick. A voice shouted, 'at last' and Esther who rushed to the man who had grabbed Nick. As she passed the first man, she elbowed him in the face, and he fell to his knees. She grabbed the second man by the hair and hit him three times with her elbow. She looked at Nick, smiled and said, 'don't want to damage my nails, only had them done this morning.' As she turned the third man took a swing at Esther which missed as she ducked down, and then sent a straight finger jab to his throat. That was followed by a side kick to the knee.

'Always go for the knee if you can, it's a very weak joint,' explained Esther.

Margret came over to Robert, with her handcuffs and said 'Robert Mills I'm arresting you for the murder of Jane Allen and Christopher Vincent. You do not have to say anything. But it may harm your defence if you do not mention when questioned something which you later rely on in court. Anything you do say may be given in evidence. 'How was that, did I get it right?'

'Fuck off.'

At that point two police cars pulled up outside the pub. Margret had anticipated what was going to happen and called it in. The look on the first officer's face was pure confusion. A Detective Sargent sitting on the floor with a bloody nose, in handcuffs being guarded by a female police office in plain clothes. Three other members of the CID were also on the ground writhing around in agony.

'PC Jarvis, what the hell's going on?' asked the policeman, who Margret recognised as PC Shanks.

'DS Mills is a bent cop and responsible for the murder of two people. Those three there were trying to interfere with a lawful arrest and were stopped by PC Barnett using the minimum of force. I think you may need to call an ambulance.'

The ambulance arrived and the injured were treated at the scene. Then they were all taken back to the police station. After a lot of confusion Nick, Esther and Margret found themselves sitting in front the Chief Superintendent, Ian Boseley.

'This is a fine mess, I've got one DS charged with murder and three other detectives that look like they've gone three rounds with Tyson Fury so, who's going to start?

Nick, Esther, and Margret just sat there looking at each other.

'At least identify yourselves,' pleaded Ian.

Margret replied, 'I'm PC Jarvis, this is PC Esther Barnett from Norfolk, who just happens to be the granddaughter of DI Philip James, who was once stationed here.'

'I remember him, a fine officer,' beamed Ian. 'And who's this Pete Waterman lookalike?'

'The names Allen, Nick Allen,' he always liked saying that.

'Where have I heard that name before?' asked Ian.

'No idea, common name.'

Esther went on to explain how on her grandfather's death bed he whispered in her ear that Jane Allen was murdered. Then after reading his diaries, she decided to try and solve the case. For the next thirty minutes, the three in turn, gave in depth details of the events leading up to today.

'And you have all the evidence?' asked Ian.

'We have compiled a file containing all the information we have gathered,' replied Margret.

'And I have his confession on my phone. I recorded it while we had a little chat,' added Nick.

'But did he actually kill Jane and Christopher?' asked Ian.

'Not sure, we think not, but he definitely arranged it,' replied Esther.

'Okay, well leave it me and I'll take it further. But I must say I very impressed, to solve a double murder that happened twenty years ago in five days, that's something. We could do with more detectives like you in St. Albans.'

'As it happens, I'm looking for a transfer and a position in CID at St. Albans would suit me down to the ground. Any chance of putting in a good word? asked Esther.

'I'll fill in my application form straight away, said Margret.'

'I've retired, but you can always call on me for a bit of consultancy work,' laughed Nick.

Once outside Nick said that he has had enough excitement for one day and was feeling tired, so he said his farewells, promised to keep in touch. With no bus due he took a taxi home. It was still light and quite warm, so he decided to spend an hour or so at *Nick's Bar* at the bottom of his garden. It didn't take long to set it up and soon he was sitting there with a pint of *Plum Porter* and a large measure of *Talisker* whisky. He'd selected to listen to a playlist called *Mood Music*. It brought back loads of memories which he enjoyed remembering. One song hit him hard, it was *Whatever Happened to the Likely Lads?* by *Highly Likely*. The one line that really hit home was "Tomorrow's almost over, today went by so fast. It's the only thing to look forward to, the past". It was when his favourite song of the week came on – Josh Groben singing *Try to Remember* (From "The Fantasticks") that it happened. He was half asleep when he noticed a black hooded figure walking towards him. When the figure reached him, Nick asked 'are you the Grim Reaper?' The figure nodded.

'Is it my time?' asked Nick.

The Reaper replied, 'soon, there's no hurry.'

'Can I ask you a question or two?'

'Of course, go ahead.'

'Where's your scythe?'

'They banned them 'Health and Safety.'

'Really?'

The Reaper gave out a scary laugh, 'no. just my little joke. Seriously, we only use it for clients going downstairs, you know, just to frighten them.'

'So, I'm going upstairs,'

'Of course, the Big Man has been impressed with you. How you've helped other people, always putting others before yourself. He's forgiven all your little indiscretions, after all you're only human.'

'You must know everything; how did DI James know my wife had been killed.'

'I told him, just before he died. I wanted to tie up loose ends.'

'That was clever of you.'

'I thought so.'

Nick was thinking hard, he wanted to clear up a few things before the end.'

'Why did people keep asking Esther if she was related to me, I mean I've never met her before.'

'Good question,' replied the Reaper. 'Do you remember that Training Course you went on at Norwich College in 1984?'

'Vaguely.'

'And you stayed in that hotel.'

'Oh yes,' said Nick, thinking back.

'Just one of the indiscretions the Big Man has forgiven.'

'Oh dear,' replied Nick. 'How long have we got?'

'I think it's time now.'

'Okay, I'm ready. Just let me finish my whisky.' He picked it up in his Summerton Club glass and finished off the last drop. It tasted like nothing else he had ever tasted – pure nectar.

'Will it hurt when I die?' he asked.

'Of course not, actually you died ten minutes ago.'

'What happens when we get there?'

'Well, they are all waiting for you, Jane, DI James, your parents, ACC Higgens, Archie Taylor, Mr Campion, and many others.

As they walked down the garden a bright light appeared in front of them with a staircase leading towards the sky. As they climbed the stairs the light faded behind them.

Bonus Story

Never Judge a Book

Never judge someone by the way he
looks or a book by the way it's covered;
for inside those tattered pages, there's
a lot to be discovered.

This story contains some adult themes.

Never Judge a Book

May 2009

There was no question whatsoever that Sara Hansford was the most desirable woman in the offices of Harris and Associates, financial advisors, where she worked as a personal assistant. She was 27 years old, five feet nine inches tall with a figure that most women would die for. She had an oval face, deep blue eyes, and an angelic smile. Her thick shoulder length blond hair was expensively cut, and her subtle make-up applied with perfection. She was also a bit of a bitch, which she always stated, *with my looks I'm entitled to be.* Unfortunately, she was also single. It's not that she didn't have lots of admirers, but none of them could measure up to her high expectations. Her last serious boyfriend was called David, although she never lived with him, they dated for nearly a year. They met in May two years ago, and for three months their relationship was everything she could wish for. He was attentive, loving and they spent those early months visiting exhibitions, going to the theatre, and eating at exotic restaurants. Then the football season began; he started playing every Saturday afternoon and Sunday mornings. During the week he couldn't see Sara on certain nights because he was either training or in the pub with his mates watching a match on Sky Sports. She used to ask him who's playing and then say, 'but that's not your team, why do you want to watch them?' He would always reply that she wouldn't understand or it's the Champions League or it's a big derby match or if England were playing, it's only once every four years. In the end. if she saw him twice a week, she was lucky, so she kicked him into touch.

Before David there was Carl, whom she lived with for two years. Carl was a good-looking lad with very good prospects in the banking business. They occasionally talked about marriage, but nothing was ever finalised. Sara thought it was only a matter of time before he popped the question. She had introduced him to her parents, and they idolised him. *You won't get a better catch* they used to tell her. She was prepared to wait. Then one evening a heavily pregnant, mousy looking primary school teacher turned up at the front door, claiming Carl was the father. Apparently, they had a one-night stand six months ago when Carl was on a stag night. Carl admitted it straight away and decided to do the right thing. According to a mutual friend they are blissfully happy, married, and living in Welwyn Garden City. Just to add insult to injury they have another child on the way.

Although she had dated a few of the better-looking men in her office, she didn't make a habit of it. She didn't want them comparing notes or be labelled the office bike. In the end they stopped asking; all of them except - Simon Watts. It was clear to most people that Simon was besotted with her. So far, he had asked her out on five separate occasions, each time she told him where to get off. He was a geek. About six foot tall, plain looking with a short haircut and thick horn-rimmed glasses. His hair, with an immaculate side parting was the sort of hair style you would find on a 1950s ten-year old boy posing for his school photo. And those ties, how she hated his ties. Last week it was Mickey Mouse and the week before Mr Spock. Together with his dull grey suit and boring shoes, he was the epitome of everything she hated in a man. This was a bit strong, as she had, apart from telling where to go, never actually spoken to him. He seemed a bit of a loner, who never really socialised with his colleagues. Last month he has asked her if she would like to accompany him to see Mamma Mia at the Prince of Wales Theatre. She just laughed in his face and told him if he was the last man on earth she would rather go on her own. At the time she was suffering from PMT and had reported him to Human Resources for sexual harassment. They said that inviting someone to see Mamma Mia did not constitute as sexual harassment, but they would have a quiet word with him. Anyway, she had already seen Mamma Mia.

Sara was deep in thought, sipping the third cup of coffee of the morning, when her thoughts were disturbed.

'Hello Sara,' said a voice behind her.

She looked round, it was him, Simon Watts; and what tie was he wearing today? Austin Powers, *who loves you baby.*

'What do you want, Simon?'

'I was just wondering if you would like to come with me to see Eric Clapton at the Royal Albert Hall on Saturday.'

Without thinking she said 'No, Simon, I would not like to see Eric Clapton with you. Don't you ever give up? Just fuck off.'

'Okay,' he replied. 'But if you change your mind, let me know.'

She shook her head and turned back to her computer. He shrugged his shoulders and walked back to his workstation.

The cheek of him, she thought, will he never take no for an answer. It suddenly dawned on her that Simon must have done his homework because Eric Clapton was her favourite artist and that particular concert had been sold out for months, and she would really like to see it. Maybe it's not too late to change her mind. No; no matter how much she would love to see Eric Clapton she was not going with Simon Watts. A lady has her standards. It was ten minutes later that she had a great idea. She remembered a film she had seen on TV last week. She wouldn't admit it to anyone, but she was a great fan of Jim Carey, and her favourite film was *The Mask.* In the film Stanley Ipkiss had tickets for some concert and he asks a girl, in the Bank in which he works, if she would like to accompany him. She manages to persuade him in parting with the tickets because she has a friend staying with her and it would be cruel to leave her at home. Great plan, she thought, I'll try it. Sara wanders over to Simon's workstation.

'Hi Simon,' she said. 'Sorry I didn't mean to be rude, I'm a bit stressed at the moment. Normally I would love to see Eric Clapton with you, but I've got an old friend from university staying with me at the weekend and I couldn't possibly leave her alone on Saturday night.'

'No problem; totally understandable,' replied Simon.

'Simon,' she said, fluttering her eye lids and giving him that look that she had perfected over many years, that seemed to get her anything she wanted. 'I was just wondering; you obviously know how much I love Eric Clapton and so does my friend Carol. Perhaps you could let me have both tickets so Carol and I could go. It would mean so much to me and I would always be in your debt.'

Simon looked into her eyes and said, 'Sorry, I know how much you like Eric Clapton but so do I. That's why I gave you first choice. I've got many friends who will bite my hand off to accompany me. Sorry.'

She turned away, cursing under her breath, and walked back to her workstation.

Over the next few days Sara's mind was in turmoil, she desperately wanted to see Eric Clapton but to be seen out with Simon Watts. It didn't bear thinking about. This dilemma lasted until Friday lunchtime when she decided that she would go with Simon to see the concert. After consuming a large portion of Humble Pie, she walked over to Simon.

'Hi Simon, how was your lunch,' she asked.

'Fine thank you, how was yours?' he replied.

'It was okay; I was just thinking, have you found anyone to accompany you to see Eric Clapton?'

'Why do you ask?'

'Well, if you haven't, I would like to accept your kind invitation.'

'What about your friend Carol?'

'Who?.........Oh, she phoned last night to say she couldn't come; flu or something.'

'Okay, that will be great. I'll book a taxi and pick you at six thirty.'

'Great,' she replied. See you then.' She turned away and went back to her workstation thinking *what have I let myself in for.*

At six thirty, Saturday evening, the bell rung at Sara's terraced cottage in Greenwich. She opened the door thinking it would be Simon.

'Can I help you?' she said looking at the handsome man standing before her. He was six foot tall with spiky hair, dressed in an Armani suit over a white tee-shirt and Paul Smith shoes. His blue eyes were even brighter than hers.

'Are you ready, Sara?' replied Simon. 'I would like to grab a drink before it starts.'

She couldn't believe the transformation. She would have never recognised him.

'Yes,' she mumbled, as she turned and nervously tripped. 'I'll just get my coat.'

They arrived in plenty of time to order two gin and tonics before the performance. Sara couldn't believe her luck as they made their way to the second row in front of the stage. During the interval they enjoyed another Gin and Tonic and discussed their favourite music. Sara was surprised how much they had in common. After the concert Simon asked Sara if she fancied something to eat as he knew a little Italian place not too far away. She was having such a great time she instantly accepted. Simon had pre-booked a taxi and within a few minutes they were entering Frankie's Italian Bar and Grill in Knightsbridge. Stepping down the stairs into a cavernous underground room brightened by wall-to-wall mirrors, red-and-white checked tablecloths, and no fewer than ten oversized disco balls, set to a soundtrack of classic lounge crooners. Then walking through to the bar to the restaurant area Simon said hello to a man Sara thought she vaguely recognized.

'Hi Marco, how are you tonight?' said Simon.

'I'm wonderful and how nice it is to see you again, Simon. And who is the delightful lady accompanying you this evening?'

'Let me introduce you. Marco, this is Sara. Sara this is Marco, the owner of this fine establishment.'

Marco took Sara's hand and kissed it, 'it's a pleasure to meet you, Sara. I hope you enjoy the rest of your evening.'

The waiter quickly found them a table and handed them menus.

'Was that who I thought it was?' asked Sara.

'Well, if you thought it was Marco-Pierre White you would be correct. He co-owns this restaurant with the jockey Frankie Dettori. I often come in here and I've become good friends with Marco.'

They ordered their food, Sara chose Prosciutto Di Palma to start with followed by Ribeye steak alla rosmarino. Simon settled for the Bresaola di Toscana followed by Ribeye steak with rucola, pecorino & vintage balsamico. This was accompanied by a bottle of Pinot Grigio Blush (Sara's choice). At the end of the evening Simon and Sara waved goodbye to Marco and waited outside the restaurant for their taxi. As they waited Sara turned to Simon and said, 'do you know a nice place where they serve coffee?'

'As it happens,' he replied. 'I've just purchased a new Tassimo.'

'Well; that settles it, back to your place.'

Simon lived in a two-bedroom flat in Falcon Wharf, with views overlooking the river. Sara fell in love with flat the second she walked through the front door. It was tastefully decorated in minimalist style and furnished with designer furniture. She adored the enlarged black and white photographs of London scenes on the wall. Although they were of familiar London sites, St Pauls, Tower Bridge etc, they were all taken from unfamiliar angles, and taken just before the sun set. She then noticed in the corner of the lounge some photographic equipment, an expensive looking camera, tripod and an assortment of lens and filters.

'Did you take these?' she asked, as he approached her with a tray two mugs of Cappuccino.

'Yes; do you like them? It's just a hobby.'

He placed the tray on the coffee table and walked towards to her.

'Shall we forget the coffee?' she asked.

He smiled as she unzipped the back of her dress allowing it fall to the floor. Then in one easy movement he picked her up and carried her into the bedroom and once there, he gently laid her on his king-sized bed. She quickly undid her bra and tossed it away revealing her exquisite 36-inch, C cup breasts. He stood there admiring the vision before him. It didn't take him long to undress, and within twenty seconds he is standing before her stark naked. She was struck dumb; standing there in front of her was the body of an Adonis, perfectly formed pecs, a complete six-pack, and thighs like Michelangelo's David. Not an ounce of fat and everything in complete proportion; except for his penis. Sticking out proud and erect; she thought it was a bit on the large size. But who's complaining? She then removed her panties exposing her immaculately waxed womanhood.

For the next three hours they made love, and he was insatiable. He could go on for ages and for the first time in her life she experienced multiple orgasms. She noticed his alarm clock showed 04:00 when he said he must have a drink. When he returned, he found her fast asleep; he smiled!

170

She woke up at about nine o'clock and wondered, for a moment where she was. Then Simon walked from the kitchen carrying a tray containing two mugs of Cappuccino.

'Hello, sleepyhead,' he said.

'Good morning gorgeous,' she replied.

He placed the tray on the bedside cabinet, he was still naked. She flung off the single sheet to expose her naked body, parted her legs and started gently rubbing herself. She knew for certain that this action would turn any man on, and she was right. She watched in wonderment as the blood rushed to his flaccid penis making it majestically rise like Tower Bridge. They made love for another hour before Simon said, 'as much as I would love to spend the rest of the day in bed with you, I have promised to take my mother for lunch; it's her birthday. She lives in Berkshire, so I need to leave soon.'

'I fully understand,' replied Sara, feeling a little disappointed.

'You go and get showered and do the other things that you have to do, and I'll make some breakfast. And maybe third time lucky for the coffee.'

Sara laughed, 'Okay darling, I really am looking forward to tasting your coffee.'

After showering, applying a little make-up and combing her hair she located her bra and dress and slipped them on. She couldn't find her knickers, but she wasn't too worried. Normally, if she thought she might get lucky, she would put a spare pair in handbag. But she had no idea what the evening was going to bring so she didn't bother. Anyway, she often went out knicker-less, especially when she was feeling particular randy. It gave her a certain sense of freedom and empowerment.

She walked into the kitchen just as Simon was plating up Eggs Royal. Two poached eggs, smoked salmon, hollandaise, served on a toasted muffin.

'Gosh, that looks good,' said Sara. 'Is there no end to your talents?'

'I'm just a modern man who likes good things,' replied Simon.

Just as Sara was (eventually) finishing her cup of delicious coffee from Simon's new Tassimo, Simon's mobile started to ring.

Simon answered it, then said, 'That's your taxi, I've paid up front. He'll take you safely home.'

Sara stood up, found her coat, and made her way to the front door. Simon opened it for her.

'Thank you so much for a fantastic evening,' said Sara, giving Simon a delicate kiss on his cheek.

'The pleasure was all mine,' replied Simon.

'You know, if there is one thing I have learnt today is, *never judge a book by its cover.*'

'Absolutely; see you at work tomorrow.'

Once settled in the taxi Sara started to reflect on her evening. Lots of questions were going through her mind. Why does he dress like a geek at work? How come he's so well off? How much does he really like me? Is he too good to be true? Could this be the man she will marry? It was the last question that really concerned her. He had been pursuing her for ages so he must like her. And he definitely ticks all the right boxes. He's tall, good-looking, great sense of humour, has style, good in bed, has contacts, loaded, and hung like a donkey. Perfect.

Sara hoped to catch Simon before they started work on Monday, but as normal, due to over-running engineering works, there were delays on the Jubilee line. She arrived at her desk at 08:25, with five minutes to spare. Simon arrived three minutes later. Monday mornings are always frantic, so there was little time for office chat. She was finding it difficult to concentrate and kept glancing towards Simon. He was also very busy, but she thought once that he glanced towards her and smiled. As the morning progressed, she noticed a lot of activity around Simon's workstation. She always thought that Simon didn't have many friends within the office, but that morning every male member of the staff had visited him. At times there was maybe two or three men chatting and laughing with him. Even colleagues from the floors above were visiting him. At about 11:30 she decided she needed a visit to the loo. As luck would have it, she had to pass Simon's workstation. When she reached his desk Simon was nowhere to be seen.

'Where's Simon?' she asked Paul Waller, who sat next to Simon.

'He's just popped upstairs for a minute; the M.D. needed a word.'

She had never seen Simon's workstation before. It was very tidy, very organised. There was just one photograph in a frame, which she assumed were his parents. It showed a good-looking middle-aged couple posing with Simon outside a rather large house. As she replaced the photo, she noticed that one of his desk draws was slightly open. She looked around and when no one was looking she opened the draw. The draw was empty except of three things. First, was a pair of knickers which she recognised as the pair she was wearing on Saturday. Second, a large bundle of twenty-pound notes. Third, a photograph of her lying in Simon's bed, asleep with the sheet neatly folded down exposing her breasts. Next to her sat Simon, complete with his horn-rimmed glasses and 1950s hair style. In one hand he was holding a mug and giving the thumbs up with the other.

'You bastard,' she screamed.

* * *

Some readers will be happy with the ending. Others like Mrs Nicklin will say what a silly ending; what really happened? So, I'm offering two endings which you can read or ignore.

Ending 1.
The Mills & Boom ending.
Sarah was mortified, she looked around, everyone was looking at her, and some were giggling, while others whispering to a colleague. She ran back to her desk grabbed her handbag, coat and ran out of the office, tears flooding her eyes. She could still hear the laughter as she left the building.

Next day Sara phoned in sick and spent the next month at home suffering from a stress related illness. She never returned to Harris and Associates. She spoke to them on the phone, and they agreed to let her go and offered a large amount of compensation.

It was six months later, after she had secured a similar position in a rival firm in St. Albans, and was starting to get her life back together, that she bumped into Simon Watts. It was a

Friday evening, and she was attending a leaving party at the *Mermaid* public house. She had only known Angela for a month, but they had become quite close. Angela was expecting a baby in two weeks' time and was taking a year's maternity leave. Sara had just paid a visit to the toilet and was making her way back to her friends when she spotted him sitting in the corner. She grabbed the nearest pint of beer, walked over to him, and poured it over his head. To her surprise he didn't react, he just looked at her and said, 'sorry.' She was transfixed and just stared back at him.

'Please, let me explain. I'm really sorry.' He beckoned her to sit down. She responded and sat down at his table without question.

For the next hour he poured his heart out to her. He explained that his parents were extremely rich and that he didn't really need to work. He had argued with them that he didn't want to marry a girl who was just after his money. So, he dressed like a geek, as she would put it, hoping to find someone who would love him for himself. He had fallen in love with her the first time he set eyes on her. But she had been so horrible to him that when his colleagues bet him that he would never bed her he accepted the challenge. He begged her to forgive him and give him another chance. She agreed.

They were married twelve months later, had three beautiful looking children, and lived happily ever after.

Ending 2
The Emily Bronte ending.

Sarah was mortified, she looked around, everyone was looking at her, and some were giggling, others whispering to a colleague. At that point Simon appeared.

'What's going on?' he enquired.

'What have you done; you've made me a laughingstock.' screamed Sara.

'I can explain, it's not what you think.'

'Not what I think. Do you think I'm stupid; you pinch my knickers, take a photograph of me, and show it to everyone. What are you some kind of sick pervert?'

'It was just a bit of fun.'

174

But she wasn't listening; she picked up an expensive looking paper knife from Simon's desk and stabbed him in the heart. Simon grabbed her and whispered, 'I love you.' As he fell to the floor she stumbled with him. As she fell, she caught her head on the corner of his desk. She let out a small scream as they collapsed together on the floor. Despite the efforts of the trained first aiders, by the time the ambulance had arrived they were both dead.

It was agreed by both sets of parents that Sara and Simon should be buried together. On many occasions it was reported in the local paper that the ghosts of a young couple were seen walking around the cemetery holding hands.

Acknowledgements

First, I must thank Russell White for encouraging me to start writing. It was in the late noughties, and I had just started my six-week summer holiday. Russell thought it would be fun, so dared me to write a book as I apparently had nothing better to do. Being a Maths teacher, English wasn't my best subject and declined the offer. After some persuasion I agreed to write a short story. We debated the content and came up with the title *Murder at the Mermaid,* (now *An Eye for an Eye)* as we were sitting in the garden of The Mermaid pub. I found writing very therapeutic as I was able combine my personal problems in a fictitious story. By the end of the summer holiday, I had written *The Scottish Ale.* The Nick Allen Mysteries had begun. These were the put aside and I started on the Young Nick Allen books, which have been a great success.

There is a selection of people who I must thank for proofreading my works at various stages, my dear wife, Janet, my daughter and son-in-law Esther and Steve. But especially Maggie Jarvis who checked on the whole book and gave me some sound advice.

And finally, a huge thanks to Mark Powell, John Cusworth and all the past and present staff of the Mermaid Public House who have served me well over the last 50+ years.

The Author

Allen Nicklin B.Ed(Hons)

The Hero

Nick Allen

The Mermaid

I first visited the Mermaid in the mid-sixties when I was a student at the Herts College of Building which was directly opposite the pub. We used to run across the road from our classroom, convince the landlord that we were of age and have a quick pint. At the time it was a Whitbread pub, which had taken over from Greens of Luton and many other pubs in the area. In the early 1990sWhitbread was required to sell almost 2500 pubs, and in 1995 the pub was briefly run by a large Leicester brewery, Everards. This association didn't work, and the Mermaid is now part of a small group called Burlison Inns, which was purchased in September 1999. Burlison specializes in serving beers from craft breweries. For many years the only regular was Citra, from Oakham Ales in Peterborough, but since has added Suffolk County from the Nethergate brewery. In 2013 the tenancy was taken up by two actors Mark Powell and John Cusworth, who have transformed the pub into one of St. Albans' favourite pub. During the COVID lockdown when drinking was eventually allowed outside, they extended the garden, and added covered pergolas. Outdoor lights and heaters were installed, and cushions and blankets are available for comfort and warmth.

In 1976 I was luckily enough to secure a teaching position at the college; therefore, the Mermaid became a lunchtime favourite. Even when my new teaching position was located in Twickenham, I made sure that I had no classes on a Friday afternoon, so I could rush back for my Friday afternoon pint. Now I've retired, the Mermaid is still my "go to" pub.

The Mermaid has won many CAMRA awards including Pub of the Year and Cider Pub of the Year. It regularly hosts beer and Cider festivals most Bank Holidays and Music every Sunday.

The Mermaid, taken from my office in 1999.

The Landlords

Mark Powell and John Cusworth

*

The Landlords (the group)

Paul Davis, John Cusworth, Paul Campany and Neil Oxtoby

The Staff

*

General Manager – Grace Simpson

Duty Manager - Ella Beedle

*

Duty Manager - James Maxwell

Assistant Manager - Danny King

*

The festivals

The Groups

Life's a Gas

*

MacLaren Wall

Katie plus Juan
*
ARC

Rouges Gallery